Larry Lockridge

Marcia Santon

OUT OF WEDLOCK

OUT OF WEDLOCK

a novel

Larry Lockridge

IGUANA

Publisher: Meghan Behse
Editor: Paula Chiarcos
Cover design and drawings: © 2020 Marcia Scanlon

ISBN 978-1-77180-564-3 (hardcover)
ISBN 978-1-77180-563-6 (paperback)
ISBN 978-1-77180-562-9 (ebook)

Out of Wedlock is a work of fiction. Names, places, events, occurrences
and incidents are either products of the author's imagination and/or used in
a fictitious manner. Any resemblances to actual persons, living or dead, or
to actual events are strictly coincidental.

This is an original print edition of *Out of Wedlock*.

to the memory of James Binkley

CONTENTS

— Part One —

THE MODERN

PYGMALION

— Chapter One —

BONES WHO DANCE

The skeletons, cracking vertebrae and knuckles as they emerged from the ground, were a vision in yellow. Jess remembered that eighteenth- and nineteenth-century victims of yellow fever, buried in Washington Square, were wrapped in yellow sheets. A few skeletons, in penitentials, had been cut down from the hangman's tree at the northwest corner. He could see fractures in the cervical vertebrae. Odd—some were sporting erections, but he knew that hominids aren't armed with penis bones.

The small clavicles of one executed offender suggested a female. This could be Rose, the young Black woman hanged in 1819 for suspected arson. She was the last to be hanged in Washington Square, which then became a military parade ground.

There were twenty-one thousand stiffs here, mostly potter's-field types. About two hundred pushed through the sod, stood upright, and began assembling close to Washington Square Arch, as if at a demo. Except they were all grinning.

Jess approached from the south as the skeletons tramped rhythmically northward and surrounded the arch. He began to sweat, for creepier than these skeletons were the two marble statues of George Washington who descended from their pediments on the arch. With slow and ponderous steps, they pushed through the encirclement of bones and set up for their gig. One carried a synthesizer, the other a set of drums.

During a recent renovation of the arch, both underwent extreme makeovers. Jess had often passed the Georges, noting how the prominent chins were weathering away, the cheeks flattening, and the lower faces displaying an embarrassing soft-tissue descent. What a challenge the Georges presented! Jess hoped the restorers wouldn't later be slapped with malpractice suits.

The makeovers seemed to have gone to the Georges' heads. What music should eighteenth- and nineteenth-century skeletons expect of them? An allemande? A minuet? A gigue? Certainly not the fusion of reggae, electro-industrial heavy metal, post-bop doo-wop, and neo-garage mojo that cleared the park of rats and pigeons. Their huge forms swayed before the arch as they competed in miking up higher and higher.

Jess felt sorry for the skeletons. They didn't know how to dance to heavy metal or neo-garage mojo. They assumed an early American formation, the longways line, male skeletons facing female, joining phalanges and metacarpals in groups of four and changing couples up and down the line. The music didn't fit, so they stumbled over one another in this dance of death, falling on the cobblestones, breaking their bones.

But after a few more minutes of deafening trash fusion, they caught on. Sternums scraped against sternums, sacra pressed against sacra, female femurs spread apart to give intimate access to one partner after another. Jess beheld a frenzy of skeletal coupling—females with males, females with females, males with males, sturdy skeletons with decrepit. A few skeletal dogs entered in, adding to the mix.

The bronze statue of Garibaldi, deliverer of Italy, strode over to find out what was going on and averted his eyes.

As a kid, Jess had learned to make a fire by rubbing twigs together. That may explain what happened next. As the skeletons humped one another and piled up like World Series champs, catastrophe was near. All at once, a feverish threesome auto-ignited near the bottom, and a conflagration spread through the heap of pathetically groping, delirious bones. A bonfire towered over Washington Square Arch, showering sparks into the empyrean. Jess panicked as the fire was engulfing him, bringing with it a mélange of partially incinerated metatarsals, fibula, tibia, and grinning toothy mandibles.

He screamed and woke up. He was not alone.

— Chapter Two —

WORLDS ELSEWHERE

Jess awakened lying in bed with two women. It had been his first go at a ménage. The women were in each other's arms and sleeping deeply when he screamed and bolted upright.

"Please, Jess, get some sleep," said one, speaking through tresses of her companion's long red hair.

"Yeah, sleep, please," said the other. "Hope you weren't having a nightmare. A good dream last night but I'm wasted. Let's sleep."

Jess knew the nightmare was triggered by the Halloween Parade the three had joined the evening before and by the party games they played. He felt too it was another visitation of dark forces from within, sent to punish him for failings from his earliest days. His mind always had it out for him—that's called having a conscience, and sometimes it seemed unfair. He made some blunders, but in his way, hadn't he always meant well, adapting the physician's credo of doing no harm, or as little as possible? Wasn't the stunning fallout from those party games punishment enough? While the two women resumed sleeping, he sat on the bedside and pondered how this chapter of his fractured life had begun.

He looked down at one of the women, the brunette. He'd met her a few years earlier, back in early October of 1989. He'd been dining alone at Café Loup on West Thirteenth Street after thirty-six hours of grisly ER stitching at St. Vincent's Hospital, where he was doing his residency. She was at a table next to him, part of a group of five with questionable manners, everybody eating off everybody else's plate. They talked about nothing except the food.

"Those escargots taste like retreads."

"Your New Zealand lamb is mutton."

"Tournedos? I'm eating wolf."

"Chocolate soufflé doesn't normally require a sharp knife."

Near the end of their meal, Jess saw an opportunity to join in and crossed the tacit boundary that protects a group of intimates from those dining alone. This was bold behavior for him. He addressed a dapper mustachioed gentleman who seemed the arbiter but whose voice was fairly high-pitched.

"Are you by chance the famed restaurant reviewer Natalia Wojciechowski?" As a facial plastic surgeon, Jess could see through disguises.

"*Feared* is more like it," replied one of her company, laughing.

"Yes, and don't blow my cover," she said. "That's against the rules."

"Rules. That's the name of a London restaurant. Ever been there?" Jess was gamely trying to hold on to the link.

"Yes, the only entrée they let you order is beef Wellington. It's always overdone and pasty."

"That was exactly my experience! My friend and I tried to order lamb chops and got talked into beef Wellington. It was overdone and pasty."

"So you don't always dine alone?"

"I have the occasional friend. Say, I remember your column on dining alone—easier for men than women, you said." In the corner he had noticed a lone young woman wearing a lustrous black wig and looking forlorn as she slowly chewed.

"Women have failed at life if they dine alone," Natalia replied. "Men are rich widowers."

"Miss Wojciechowski will not ask if *you* are one," put in one of her cohort, an epicure with girth sufficient for two armchairs. "I too would rather not know. But perhaps you'd like to join us?" He put out a meaty hand. "I'm Horace Holliday." The others introduced themselves as well.

Jess pulled up a chair next to Natalia Wojciechowski for the coffee service. It was the beginning of a long-lived affair.

* * *

Born of unknown parentage in Santa Fe in 1962, Jess grew up in the care of a series of foster parents who always returned him to the Albuquerque agency within a few months, like defective merchandise. The agency wasn't particular about placing its wards. Prospective foster parents would undergo a review less severe than given a young married couple seeking a stray at Bideawee. So Jess confronted an odd assortment of faux siblings and parents over the years.

"My earliest memories are of *Ma*drid—that's a ghost town south of Santa Fe . . . Yeah, accent on the first syllable. My foster parents were hippies who refurbished an old miners' shack and paid for their bean sprouts by selling turquoise and pottery—as if the Indians didn't do them better."

Jess and Natalia had just had late-afternoon sex during their first assignation, three weeks after their initial meeting. By his standards it hadn't gone all that badly. Natalia had even orchestrated a finale without precedent in his own limited repertoire. So he was feeling talkative as they lay in bed sipping Château Gloria. She brought along the wine and some foodstuffs to his bare resident's quarters on West Fifteenth Street, and he supplied a candle.

"My primal scene was watching my foster parents have group sex in arroyos. I played by myself, shaping sand into body parts. When the commotion died down, they'd take me back to the shack and whip me with piñon branches."

"Ouch. Poor kid. Did your years in Madrid color your view of sex?" Natalia rolled over, her rear displayed to advantage in the candlelight, and grabbed for the goose liver pâté.

"Afraid so. I didn't understand what they were doing but it looked silly and I linked it with punishment. Escaped when they returned me to the agency covered with welts and fleabites, no questions asked."

"Who was next?"

He sighed. "Not much better. Swinging bisexuals from Santa Barbara. They wore plaid Bermuda shorts and ran a hair salon in Santa Fe. Always upbeat about the bisexual lifestyle—so I came to hate the word *lifestyle*. Sent me to kindergarten in plaid Bermuda shorts and a perm—long curly red hair that stank of chemicals. The other kids made fun of me. In the evening, swinging couples would come over for barbecued sausage and Mateus rosé. They frugged and smoked pot and went off to the bedroom while my three foster siblings played Dirty Doctor. I stayed out of that game and shaped little figurines from whatever I could find on the floor."

"Not much better."

"Later there were Chicanos from Cerrillos wanting the agency stipend. You know Cerrillos, some forty miles south of Santa Fe? Last I heard, it still has only three hundred inhabitants—Chicanos, hippies, a few Indians, and every household has a vicious dog. They made *Young Guns* there a couple of years ago, and the town voted to keep the movie façades. You walk through swinging doors to a nineteenth-century saloon and find yourself in a discount drugstore."

"That's got to be some sort of metaphor." Natalia chomped on a cornichon.

"Yeah, and here's another. My foster dad was devoted to his junk car. If we visited a neighbor, he ordered the whole family into the old Thunderbird, drove two hundred feet and we piled out. Using the car was a cultural must. All Chicanos in town did it. One morning before sunrise, he returned me to the agency in the Thunderbird. Foster mom didn't come along."

"This is getting very sad. Who tried you out next?" She pressed an olive to his lips.

"Believe it or not, I spent six months on an Indian reservation. Nothing but shacks and the occasional teepee in back for the kids. I tried to make a go of it and was good at carving female wooden effigies but still got returned to the agency."

"Okay, I get the picture," she said, sitting up and taking measure. "But you're smart, no obvious deformities, you're even white. What was wrong with you?"

Jess frowned. "Well . . . I had what psychiatrists call spontaneous eidetic imagery. Whether it's a disorder or a special power, I'm not sure. Someone once told me I was just like William Blake. As a kid I'd go into a trance for hours, sometimes escaping things, sometimes making real something I wanted, but it was always a waking dream. The scene was fully tangible, with a cast of characters who appeared and reappeared. Most kids outgrow it by the time they're six. I didn't . . ." He looked away from her. "Still happens from time to time but just for moments."

Natalia's eyes widened as Jess continued in an intense whisper. As he told her about his trances, he slipped into one again. *There was a mentor with a large nose, very wise like a patriarch. He was teaching me a secret ritual to ward off evils. There was a priestess— eyes snake-green like a lamia, hair brilliant red. I wanted to please her, to be held by her before she faded. And there were sisters, brothers, playmates. We'd run around a village with thatched roofs instead of desert shacks and teepees, until our play was stopped by kindly elders. They all faded. Farewell, farewell, everlasting farewells!*

Jess looked up at Natalia and shook his head, snapping to. "Then I'd step out of my trance into real life in Madrid, Cerrillos, the reservation—the sound of carburetors and dogs barking. I'd go from being out of touch to being out of sync. I also had nightmares, really terrible. I'd scream and wake everybody up. Still do, sometimes. You might say all my foster parents and siblings got pissed at me. Can't blame them . . . And that's what was wrong with me, Natalia."

Offering a dried apricot, she said, "Thanks for the heads-up about those trances. I'll be on the lookout. But how do you get from eidetic imagery and botched foster care to plastic surgery and dining alone at Café Loup?"

"Easy. My final set of foster parents ran a mom-and-pop funeral home next to the municipal library in Santa Fe. A brisk business, what with all the fatalities on US 285. While they were busy plastering over rips and tears and turning grimaces into smiles, I'd play hooky and sneak next door to read. All day long. I could read books and go into trances at the same time. Had a cast of imaginary friends who sat around and read with me. The librarians ignored me—was researching some school project or other, I'd tell them. Flunked out of high school, hardly ever showed up. There were so many truants in Santa Fe in those days that I fit right in. Was self-taught—picked up vocabulary and calculus and geography all on my own. Also some anatomy, but the graphics turned up in my nightmares. It wasn't because I flunked out—I got returned because I went into trances at dinner. My foster parents were avid cooks and I never saw them wash their hands when they left their cadavers. And it's hard to eat when you know there's a stiff in the next room. I preferred being in a trance. Had lost lots of weight in the two years I was there, but the agency didn't ask any questions when my mortuary pop dropped me off. My foster mom stayed home to tend a corpse."

"I see—plastic surgery is a way of continuing your foster parents' profession but on the living? Or so it seems . . . Well, how did you arrive at St. Vincent's?"

"To get me off their hands, the agency supplied me with a fake high school equivalency diploma and forced me to take the SATs. I scored a perfect sixteen hundred and off I went to Harvard on full scholarship. As a kid, my mind had somehow been accessing words and numbers even while going off into its own green world. Remember, I had my wise mentor there. The hours I clocked at the library paid off. I'd spent lots of time in the company of compromised bodies even before I ended up at the mortuary, so I declared for pre-med and graduated in three years. Then on to Harvard Medical School, where I opted for plastic surgery. As a kid I spent hours making and shaping things—did I mention the human figures of Silly Putty I bounced off the noodles of my peers? My way of trying to make friends, I guess. And I'd watched my foster parents make corpses look glam. All this entered in, I'm sure."

"Jess, don't you ever wonder about your *real* parents?" asked Natalia. "Seems to me they owe you one, throwing you at the mercy of all those weirdoes."

Jess looked askance. He was always ill at ease when somebody raised the question of his biological parents and had various ways of dodging it. "Yes, it's an enigma. Who the Sam Hill am I? Was I born out of wedlock or were the creeps married? Well, I don't care if I'm a bastard but I'd be really put out to learn they were Republicans."

"I hear you, but you're a physician and maybe you've heard about genetics. Wouldn't you like to have some things explained, like this William Blake syndrome of yours? Where'd that come from?"

"Thanks for asking, but let's put my parents on hold. You've got my story, Natalia. What's yours?"

Chapter Three

NATALIA'S STORY

"We don't have much in common, Jess. I know my biological parents all too well. I'm Polish—God only knows what you are. I'm religious. Not Ivy League. I'm wary of doctors and go to homeopaths and chiropractors. And I know more about sex."

"Uh-oh."

She laughed. "Just kidding, you're not half bad."

"Well, from a food reviewer, that's a relief." But Jess was suddenly embarrassed about being naked and pulled up the sheet.

"They call me 'Chow-ski' back in the kitchens, circulate photos of me caught in disguises. The thing about being found out is the food gets better. The entrées are superior to the appetizers, but then I don't get a real take. It's all fakery. I get the only fresh Dover sole in the icebox. The waiters may all be out-of-work actors, but they can't hide that they know that I know that they know. So I try not to be found out."

"Have you always been a food reviewer?"

"You might ask how many Polish Americans end up with my job. We're all raised on kielbasa and pierogi, lard and communion wafers, right?"

"Well, were you?"

"Actually, yes. And recipes out of Lucyna Cwierczakiewiczowa."

"Beg your pardon?"

She smiled. "Don't you know anything, Jess? Cwierczakiewiczowa wrote the first Polish cookbook. My mother held on to her culture. We spoke Polish around the house. She kept us from eating American junk food or processed crap. Ahead of her time, that girl. Instead of Campbell's tomato soup, we had *czernina*—that's duck-blood soup, and *golonka*—that's stewed pork knuckle, and *flaki*—that's tripe stew with marjoram. Neighbors complained about the smell. My siblings and I—Jesus, we were mortified! We envied the kids who got Nathan's hotdogs—but we got real food."

"Nothing that could turn the stomach of an ER resident. What was your neighborhood?"

"Tompkins Square, of course. There were lots of Polish restaurants in those days. Not anymore." She looked out the window. "Hey, let's hop a cab over there. Sentimental journey. Tom's working late tonight. I've got some extra time. We can walk back to Bethune Street after. I like walking, check out new restaurants along the way."

"Tom?"

"The guy I live with. Tom Langley."

"Oh." Jess noticed early on that Natalia had a way of assuming prior knowledge of personal details the way kids do.

"We've been living together two years now. We don't see much of each other during the week, so we make it a rule to have sex every other Saturday morning. Whether we need it or not."

They got out at Seventh Street and Avenue A. Natalia pointed to some fourth-floor windows of a yellow brick apartment building. It was drab and squat. "I used to look out those three dirty windows onto the park. There were dozens of old Polish and Ukrainian widows sitting on benches in black woolen coats, even in summer. No iron fences in those days, so the grassy areas were filled with hippies and junkies. I tell people I saw Abbie Hoffman wrap himself in an American flag—maybe that's a false memory . . . Anyway, the widows and hippies got along well enough. The widows were high on second-hand smoke. Whenever I smell pot it's a nostalgia trip. I'm right back here in Tompkins Square and it's the late sixties."

"Where was your father in all this?"

"Oh, he was here, sort of. Emigrated shortly after my mother— they met in a church basement. His great ambition was to start a Polish American newspaper, something local. Called it the *Polish Plainsong*. It started well enough, but then his subscribers began dying off. He'd go to the storefront on East Sixth and there'd be a copy of the *Plainsong* with 'Deceased, return to sender.' My mother was a cleaning lady for Upper East Side Jews, or we couldn't pay the rent. Only ninety-five a month in those days. My father almost never spoke to me. By the end of the day he was in a vodka haze. I'd try to get his attention by using Catholic schoolboy talk I'd overheard, like 'badadapoopie' or 'Eat my salami.' Or I'd break some household rule, like messing around with his shaving equipment— and I'd feel guilty about it. He spent two hours every morning prepping for a day of disappointment."

"So what became of him?" By now they had walked the circular paths into the park's interior and were near the neoclassical Temperance Fountain. At the top of the four marble columns stood Hebe, mythical water carrier, set there to persuade the thousands of local drunks to give up booze.

"I think he slipped rat poison onto his pierogi . . . No, I really do. They kept bags of the stuff near the park office. He died after dinner. He was thirty-nine, I was seven. No autopsy. They said it was a heart attack, but his final words were, 'Don't tell the pope.' For a Catholic to kill himself is a no-no. The priest curses your corpse. You get sent to hell for all eternity."

"Do you believe in that sort of thing?"

"Jess, I know we just fooled around, but why do you think you can ask me all these personal questions?" She laughed.

He cleared his throat. "Well, don't *take* them personally."

"The short answer is yes." They were walking toward the southeast corner of the park. "See that school building? St. Brigid's.

That's where I learned to be a naughty Catholic schoolgirl. I'm still trying. I believe in rules, I break the rules."

"No fun breaking rules you don't believe in."

"Mostly I keep the rules."

"So you are still a . . . a Catholic?" He found it almost as hard as saying *Jew*.

"Yes. The Sisters of Mercy drilled me with Jesus and Mary, and the Pauline Fathers sealed them in for good. It's a cliché, but the nuns had us so aware of sin and temptation that we thought about sex all the time. I remember squirming in my pleated skirt. Come on, I'll show you where I went to mass—I still do every Sunday morning, same place."

They walked west to 101 East Seventh Street and stood before the St. Stanislaus Bishop & Martyr Church. "See, the sign lists four Sunday masses, three in Polish. I go to the eight a.m. Polish mass, so I keep up the language and the faith at the same time."

"It says confession is Saturdays, four to five. I guess you go every other week?"

"Jess, it's not just that my sex life is illegitimate, it's my whole life. Every other Saturday I beg for forgiveness, not just for sex. It's for everything I am."

"So maybe both of us are illegitimate, you for misbehaving, I for being born out of wedlock, a bastard."

"Out of wedlock . . . I think of *wedlock* and for me it means getting locked into marriage, and I'd rather stay out of it. By my age—I'm thirty-one, your elder—all good Polish American girls are locked into marriage. My three sisters are in Buffalo spawning away and feeling sorry for me, but I'm the only one with a real career and not beaten by a jerk. My mother gives me lots of grief. So do the priests."

"Oh, she's still living?"

"Of course. Polish mothers never die while they have an unmarried daughter. She's in an old folks' home in the Bronx and calls me every day, four or five times, always asking if I'm engaged yet. Tom's not permitted to pick up the phone in his own house because I'm afraid it might be Mom. She's never approved of Tom—he's a rough-and-ready Australian—she pretends he doesn't exist. I rarely mention him."

"Does she know you live together?"

"Yes and no. What she hopes she doesn't know won't hurt her."

Still on East Seventh, they were passing McSorley's Old Ale House. "Let's duck in here a minute," she said. "On principle."

"Principle?"

"Yes, you know the feminists went to the Supreme Court in 1970 to get women admitted here. Oldest Irish pub. It's like earning the right to vote—women earned it, so they ought to vote. And they ought to drink here. Too bad it's turned into a tourist joint and fraternity hangout. See that wanted poster for John Wilkes Booth? Fitting because Lincoln drank ale here when he spoke at the Cooper Union across the way."

"Wasn't that the speech that turned the election?"

"Yes, and McSorley's claims Abe drank the ale *before* his speech. So this bar takes credit for the Lincoln presidency." She glanced up at the waitress. "One light, one dark, and a bowl of chili with two spoons, please." She took a sip and set her beer mug down. "Here I can be myself since the only food they serve is chili and hamburgers. Don't tell anybody, Jess, but this is the food I really want."

"Lips sealed. Now then, a serious topic . . . Have you heard that Lincoln was gay?"

"Of course, and it makes sense. The last thing in the world he wanted was to marry Mary Todd. He tried to back out. Was in love with that hayseed who told him he had perfect thighs. Mary's the one I feel sorry for. No wonder she went nuts. Now they're blaming her for the assassination, you know. It was women who carried derringers in those days, and she owned one. If John Wilkes Booth had been a serious assassin, why would he use a lady's pistol with a single bullet? Mary had the motive, she had the weapon, the opportunity."

"This adds a twist to the old joke... Well, I guess it was a miserable marriage."

"Most are, don't you think?"

He sighed. "Oh, I don't know. Maybe our sample groups are skewed—your father escaped wife and family with rat poison, most of my foster parents were into weirdo sex, the Lincolns were a sorry misfit. How can we make generalizations?"

As they were chatting and scooping up chili, Jess looked over to the corner with a wishbone lamp not far from Houdini's cufflinks. There sat a young woman with a strikingly long and narrow face, wearing a lustrous red wig, drinking alone and looking anxious. Had he seen her somewhere before?

They finished eating and walked down Astor Place to Waverly and over to the Washington Square Arch.

"Jess, my real calling is tour guide. Do you know the story behind the arch?"

"Can't say I do." This was the first time he noticed that the chins on the two George Washingtons were crumbling.

"Another miserable marriage, another murder," she said.

"Don't tell me Washington was assassinated!"

"Not Washington. Stanford White, New York's greatest architect. He designed the arch to commemorate the one hundredth anniversary of Washington's inauguration—originally wood, but they liked it so much it got converted to marble. Stanford White is all over town. He designed the Century Club, the Players Club, the Bowery Savings Bank, even that church across the park. Also mansions uptown and on Long Island for Gilded Age millionaires. Bedrooms with double doors so guests could make as much noise as they liked. And there were double corridors so they wouldn't be confronted by frowning chambermaids."

"Why would anybody bump him off? Disgruntled client?"

"How can you not know the story? White was the world's biggest letch. He had a suite at the top of the old Madison Square Garden. Designed it himself and had a red velvet swing attached to the ceiling.

That's where he seduced dozens of showgirls. His wife looked the other way. One of the girls was Evelyn Nesbit, totally gorgeous. He debauched her when she was seventeen—slipped something into her punch and she woke up undone. Then she married a rich bully named Harry Thaw. He beat her on their honeymoon when he found out she wasn't a virgin. She told him about White."

Jess spontaneously imagined Natalia on the red velvet swing with Stanford White.

She turned over so he'd have easy access to her gilded ass as the swing moved languidly through space.

One of his spells was coming on, when he'd be transported to his other world. He knew to take measures, especially when stitching people up in the ER, so he leaned against the arch to bring himself back.

"Then what happened?"

"Big party in the Garden one night, summer of 1906. White was sitting at the table closest to the showgirls. A performer was singing 'I Could Love a Million Girls,' and up walked Thaw in a heavy black overcoat."

"Like a Polish widow?"

"Not quite—and don't interrupt. He pulls out a revolver and shoots White three times in the face. At first everybody thought it was a party trick. Thaw politely removed the remaining bullets from his gun to let people know they should continue partying. They tried, but the performers soon lost heart with a bloody corpse at their feet. Thaw escaped the chair with an insanity plea—the first in history. He spent a short time in jail, catered by Delmonico's. We should go there sometime to see if the beef has held up. I'll wear my gangster disguise."

"As a rule I thought people are jealous about something happening right under their nose, not affairs that happened years ago."

"I'm not jealous about what's happening even under my nose. I never get jealous."

"Oh."

"And if you must know, I've never been in love. Everybody blames it on my father. I don't blame him a bit. It frees up lots of energy for other things. People in love are crazy, consumed—they get nothing done, they lose their jobs, they develop eating disorders and commit crimes of passion, like Thaw. They stalk."

"I'm no psychologist, but I'll bet that was a crime of *ego*. Uh, did you just say *they stalk*?"

"Yeah, they stalk. Everybody knows that."

"Oh."

They neared Sixth Avenue and turned right. After majoring in communications at Fordham, Natalia had worked two years as an apprentice cultural reporter in downtown Manhattan for the *New York Times*. Part of her job was learning the history of Greenwich Village.

"The face of the Village is always changing, you know, but somehow it holds on to its identity, despite Sixth and Seventh Avenues. They didn't go below Eleventh Street until the early twentieth century, then they gouged their way through the smaller streets."

They turned west on Christopher Street and sat on a doorstep while Natalia gave him an impassioned account of Village lore. Of how up through the early seventeenth century the Canarsee Indians called the area Sapokanican, an aromatic sandy marshland with scattered hills and a trout stream where they fished, trapped beaver, and grew tobacco. Of how the Dutch swindled them out of their island with a handful of tchotchkes, and Governor Wouter van Twiller claimed the area as his personal tobacco plantation. Of how the English then sent the Dutch packing in the later seventeenth century and began an era of genteel country living in hilltop mansions like Warren House and Richmond Hill. Of how the English were in turn sent packing by the American Revolutionaries like George Washington, John Adams, Alexander Hamilton, and Aaron Burr, who helped themselves to Warren House and Richmond Hill.

Of how Greenwich Village then became the refuge whenever smallpox or yellow fever, brought in by shipping vessels, took hold two miles south in the Battery, and the country estates gave way to a labyrinth of small streets as the population expanded. Of how in 1841 the Village was exempted from the austere street grid of the city planners, with the farsighted goal of confusing tourists, who still can't grasp how West Fourth Street can intersect West Tenth.

Of how this peaceable kingdom always had a gift for riots, from the Civil War draft riot to Stonewall. But the riot to end all was the Astor Place Riot of 1849. Twenty-two people were killed over the question of whether William Macready, an Englishman, or Edwin Forrest, an American, was the better Shakespearean actor.

"I'd rather lose my life in a cause than a plague," interjected Jess finally as they got up and walked on. They passed the Oscar Wilde Memorial Bookshop and stood outside Stonewall Tavern. "AIDS is one plague you don't escape by taking a carriage ride two miles from Battery Park to Greenwich Village. It holed up *in* the Village. Look at this street—it's depopulated like a ghost town. Hardly anybody even in the Stonewall."

"I remember Christopher Street in the seventies," said Natalia. "I'd sneak over here at night with other Catholic schoolgirls just to watch the parade of male flesh. I remember the tight jeans, small mustaches, the T-shirts and closely cropped hair. The summertime gay uniform then. We knew what they did with each other was an abomination in the eyes of God. The nuns told us it was sodomy! Problem was, some of my friends were protecting their virginity by giving blow jobs and having anal sex."

"Those poor nuns worked so hard to keep you pure and intact."

"Intact, yes . . . So, Jess, now I'm entitled to a personal question. Did you ever swing that way?"

"You mean gay? No, can't say that I have. I woke up once during foster-care days being fondled by a Seventh-day Adventist. It didn't take. I seem to be narrowly hetero." Silence. He failed to seize the moment and ask about her own same-sex proclivities. Instead, tritely, "How did you discover your own body?"

"The wavy floor-length mirror we had in the bathroom, but I didn't take a good look until I was about fourteen."

"Was that when you discovered your . . . your ass?"

"Yes, I took a good look at it from all angles, like a contortionist. The boys made fun of me and I felt it must be a liability. But I soon learned better."

Jess felt a trance coming on. *Natalia was standing naked as a teenage girl looking at her body in the mirror. He longed to touch and repossess that body through all the time forever lost to him. Then, transformed into a younger girl, she was smiling at him, wearing a Catholic girl's uniform as they played on the school ground during elementary school recess. She turned around, beckoned to him, and ran off, climbing the jungle gym. She hung upside down, her undies showing. Young Jess felt he should avert his eyes. She faded into the jungle gym. Farewell, farewell!*

He snapped out of the trance in time not to fall off the sidewalk's edge at Hudson Street and reflected more studiously on Natalia's face and body. Stunning more than beautiful, she had high cheekbones and an elegantly pointy nose, like many Poles, and a certain hauteur in eyes and brows and lips. She had a narrow back and shoulders, small breasts with eloquent nipples, slender arms, and a tiny high waist. Undercutting the upper-body restraint was a derriere so audacious that Jess assumed many pedestrians would take a block's detour. Her contours were all the more enticing for the loose-fitting black linen slacks she wore this evening.

But he'd noticed during their assignation that she had funny-looking feet, flat with premature bunions and toes going in all directions. She told him later that an Old World East Village cobbler made her footwear to order—she refused to go to a podiatrist. They appeared to Jess like sturdy old-lady shoes, not the fuck-me's you'd expect. Without them, she couldn't take long urban walks. She blamed her feet on her ass—they were stressed from girding up the remarkable apparatus.

"Yes, I'm sure you've gone through life with admirers," Jess said. But Natalia frowned and was silent. "Sorry, did I misspeak?" he asked.

"Not your fault, it's just the idea of... *admirers.* I speak sometimes at colleges on how successful women have marketed themselves. Someone I met there has been stalking me recently. Jess, look, I'm in a good mood. I don't want to talk about it."

"Fine."

Turning north onto Hudson, they passed Ophelia's, a lesbian bar. "I hear men can drop in on these places. Want to be my escort?" he asked jauntily. In reality he was regretting that he would soon drop her off and she'd bed down with another man.

"Sorry, no time, must get back to fix Tom his supper." They lapsed again into silence as they walked up Hudson to Bethune and took a left. "We live around the corner from Westbeth. As you must know, it's a very arty neighborhood."

Jess cringed at the *we.*

"But there's lots of hooker action down at Washington and West, and leather bars," Natalia said. "So thanks for walking me to the door. Do you want to meet Tom?"

Jess had been worried about bumping into Tom and duking it out. "Please, Tom," he'd say as he dodged a giant Australian fist, "sorry, but really, nothing happened." He didn't think he could look Tom in the eyes only a few hours after having some fairly weird sex with the man's girlfriend.

"Thanks a lot, Natalia, but do you mind if I take a rain check? I'm bushed."

"Fine. See you soon, maybe in a couple of weeks." She deftly kissed the tip of his nose and disappeared through the portal of the well-appointed townhouse.

— Chapter Four —

MISMATCHES

When Jess finished his residency a year later, he took a modest one-bedroom apartment on Carmine Street, joined a nearby physicians' group practice, and set about repaying his hefty student loans. The southwest district of Greenwich Village, long known as Little Sicily, had seen, by the early nineties, a loss of Italian pork stores to food emporiums but still sported enough bakeries, social clubs, and gangster restaurants to retain its ethnic identity. Jess's landlady, Mrs. Cimenti, who occupied the ground apartment, was from the old country. She didn't believe in heat after 8:00 p.m. This guaranteed a rapid turnover of tenants with blue lips and chattering teeth. High blood pressure, too, since neither civic codes nor sweet reason prevailed over Mrs. Cimenti's conviction that heat after 8:00 p.m. was *insopportabile.*

Up the block, at Father Demo Square, stood the imposing bell tower of Our Lady of Pompeii, frequently in its dirge mode as the old parishioners died off. Every July, the Festa Italiana, sponsored by the cathedral, left enough stinking debris in its wake to incur stiff fines by the Department of Health, which in deference to local gangsters knew to deliver the summonses with a wink and a nod. For the three years that Jess lived there, the church never picked up the debris.

The apartment was less bare than his quarters while a resident. There was a beanbag chair of seventies vintage but in mint condition, sundry artifacts from New Mexico on the mantel of a working fireplace, a fake Tiffany lamp in the kitchen, art purchased pre-framed and on the cheap at the Annual Village Art Fair, and a Spanish dresser he carried piece by piece from an antiques store on Hudson Street. It had a mirror that made people appear skinnier and, at Natalia's urging, he placed it across from the queen-sized bed he got through Dial-a-Mattress.

During his years on Carmine Street, he continued seeing Natalia, who set the rules of their relationship. So that he would not overestimate her own involvement—and maybe, he flattered himself, so she herself would not get too involved—she saw him only once every two weeks, late Thursday afternoons, even when Tom was out of town.

One afternoon she arrived with sex gadgets from Toys in Babeland. His job was to keep them clean and at the ready. She permitted herself two vibrator orgasms per visit. Maybe more would have given him the wrong idea.

Gradually, in post-sexual stupors, they shared stories of their earlier sex lives. Jess would worry the next day that both had blabbed too much.

"You've been good not to ask why we do only oppositional sex—that's my term for it," Natalia said. "Want to know?"

"All ears."

"Well, a year before I met you, Tom found out I was having sex with an upstate beekeeper whenever he came in to sell honey at the Union Square farmers market."

"How'd he find out?"

"Read my diary, of course. Then he wanted to know what this beekeeper had that he didn't. The answer should have been clear enough from the diary."

Jess didn't ask.

"He threatened to kick me out."

"I guess Aussies aren't so liberated as Americans." Jess professed the standard New York male liberality in such matters.

"He told me I had to stop having sex with the beekeeper, so I promised."

"I read somewhere that sex promises are out of fashion."

"They are. But Tom forgot to throw in a ban on having sex with anybody else in the universe. And somebody else came along—a performance artist from Tribeca. My promise to Tom didn't cover him, but I confess it felt like a sophistry. So I decided not to have literal *sex*—you know, intercourse—only oppositional sex. I'd discovered it at my club, the New York Institute for the Humanities. Our Friday lunches were often crashed by a subway harpist in her early nineties. PBS did a ten-minute special on her, maybe you saw it. She would tell us about an encounter with Salvador Dali in Rome as a young woman. He wanted to have sex but only if they sat in opposite corners of the bedroom and did self-service. You know, sex without actually having sex. She said she always regretted turning him down, but we told her it made for a better story."

"So we haven't been having sex?"

"Of course not. If Tom were to find out, I could look him in the eyes and say, 'I haven't had sex with that man!'"

"What about the sex toys?"

"Those don't count. Could Tom really think I'd leave him for a vibrator?" She looked dismissively at the paraphernalia on her corner cushion.

"And all our preliminary stuff? Making out and saying things— you know, *foreplay*?"

"That's not real sex."

"I'm not going to argue you out of this, but have to say, Nattie, some would disagree."

She laughed. "Okay, it's drawing a fine line, but that's how I've kept my promise."

Nervously, "And do you still keep a diary?"

"Yes, but now it's in mirror-reversed Polish script, and I've found a better place to hide it."

Whenever it was his turn, Jess talked about how his romantic life had been mostly an ordeal of yearning. The few girls who entranced him eluded him. In third grade in Santa Fe, he'd met Alison, a cross-eyed girl with long blonde hair. After school he would follow her to her adobe house on De Vargas Street piping on his tonette and offering to carry her books. He never quite caught up with her—if he got within a foot or two she'd scoot forward like a negatively charged toy bug. Over the years he kept up his quest, sending fifty-cent valentines, sitting behind her in school and brushing his knuckles against her sand-encrusted hair, walking by her house on the chance she'd be coming out the door to walk the family armadillo—and he'd pretend to be just sauntering by. But she never came out.

Jess told of years of disappointment in his quest for Alison. Eventually they became friends. She'd drop him postcards from wilderness areas around the country while she worked for the Sierra Club or call him from time to time when he was at Harvard Medical School to ask if he knew of a reputable dermatologist near Mount St. Helens or a trustworthy gynecologist in Saskatchewan.

In August 1989, just weeks before he met Natalia, he got a call from her. A seat had opened up on a canoeing expedition down the Green River in Utah, and could he be in Moab by noon the next day?

"On impulse I said yes. This meant I'd be missing out on a week of blepharoplasty, rhytidectomy, and otoplasty. But I took a chance. I didn't know anything about canoeing, and the first day out we hit the only white water of the entire trip. I looked pathetic up front, while a beefy Mormon in the rear—"

"You mean you were in the bow and he was in the stern?"

"Yes, bow, stern . . . Nattie, isn't it enough that I can name every bloody part of the human body? Anyway, this Mormon did the work of steering the thing and Alison sat in the middle watching my futile paddling. We reached the first landing late afternoon and I hoped to bed down with her under the stars, in the same sleeping bag. You know, Gary Cooper and Ingrid Bergman. What the devil was I thinking? There were some fifteen other people on the expedition. She slept alone in her own tent, while I parked my sleeping bag on an air mattress every night out in the open, as close to her tent as was seemly. I warded off tarantulas and listened to snoring from neighboring tents."

Natalia shook her head sympathetically. "So you go all the way to the Green River and wish you had earplugs?—We could use them right now, the Festa is heating up—But go on, what happened next?"

"We got to the confluence with the Colorado after six days and nights of torture. It was during the Perseid meteor shower. I'd lie on my back watching shooting stars until dawn. That evening, she asked if we could walk around the river's fork. I thought maybe she'd now confess her love, but no. She'd been going with this guy in the forestry service—he was usually on these expeditions but was having back problems from pumping iron. He wanted me to fill in for him. Ha! A naïve macho just asking to be replaced. But no, he had a problem. 'Yes, go on,' I said hopefully. 'Well, he has another physical issue, it's a little embarrassing . . . You see, he's got a nose that just doesn't quit.' And would I drop by when we got back and give him a quickie in a local clinic? Maybe at a reduced rate since I was only a resident."

"So did you do it?" asked Natalia.

"Yes, with an absent-minded supervisor looking on. Botched it a little and flew back to Boston the next day in a funk. I thought of giving up on romance the way others give up on life." He sighed.

"Jess, this is such a sad story, like all the others you've been telling me. But it shows I'm right about being in love. It drives even sensible people like you crazy."

Jess pondered this as he stood in his boxers next to the window. *Maybe she's right—I should stop falling in love.* He stared out at the Ferris wheel that was always parked by Our Lady of Pompeii in front of his apartment house during the Festa. A long-faced woman in a cottony blonde wig was riding alone. Her eyes met his for a few seconds, and then again for seven turnings of the wheel. Fearing he was headed for a trance, he shut the blinds.

Yes, Natalia had a point about love. And beyond insanity there were some crummy ironies in the romantic life. She was hardly a sexual predator, but Jess's notches were considerably fewer than hers. He suspected the unimpressive record was owing in part to his being a good conversationalist. Women told him they valued his company and didn't *want* sex. After the usual six months, the relationship would go bust and they'd be out a good dinner companion.

"Women tell me they sometimes have sex with bores on first dates because it's the only way to liven up a dull evening. But I wait around for months or years."

"With us, Jess, I wanted sex right away, oppositional that is, didn't want to wait around. It was your nerve in breaking into our dinner party—and the correct pronunciation of my name."

He told her he usually lacked that kind of nerve. But sometimes impulse overrode timidity—and then it was as if his life were being lived for him, as if he were taking dictation from another world. Natalia was like a gift for his acting on impulse.

"Too bad I can't *try* to be more impulsive."

"Yes you can, and I have a suggestion. All this talk of canoeing reminds me of something I've been meaning to ask you. Tom's great passion isn't for me, you know. It's for sailing. He says we should all go sometime—you bring along that girl you've been dating."

"*He* suggested it? This sounds too much like the story I just told."

"I'm afraid if we don't he might wonder why. I talk about you all the time. Come on, be impulsive. Let's go sailing!"

Jess was seeing an Austrian woman named Ethelinda on occasion to fill in the two-week gaps as he awaited another visit from Natalia. She lived in Brooklyn with her Brazilian paramour, an importer of stolen archeological artifacts from Guatemala. From

Ethelinda's chitchat, it didn't take Jess long to figure out the daisy chain. The Brazilian was having it off with his Guatemalan secretary, who was living in sin with a Jewish haberdasher in Queens, who was having an affair with an English milliner in the East Village, who was fooling around with her Serbo-Croatian handyman, who was having sex with virtually everybody, including Ethelinda, and so we come full circle.

Ethelinda and Jess had met at his office when she presented noisily with what proved to be not an aortic aneurysm but a heavy period. She took a liking to Jess when he alone among the physicians didn't snicker. "Better safe than sorry," he said.

Ethelinda was in the Austrian sausage–import business. Tom Langley thought she and Natalia would have lots to talk about regarding food. He didn't know just how much he had in common with Jess, and Ethelinda didn't know how much she shared with Natalia. None of this could they talk about.

Tom was in the real estate business, having sailed to New York from Perth as a young adventurer out to make his fortune. This he did handily enough through a stroke of luck. When the city ran a lottery on some properties in default on taxes, he bought a decrepit Greenwich Village townhouse for a dollar, fixed it up, and sold it for a fortune. This permitted him to buy other townhouses, trading up and getting rich. Though in his late fifties, he was on the recent list of 100 Most Eligible Bachelors in New York City. Natalia expressed no qualms. The photograph featured him on his yacht, the *Spirit of Parmelia.*

* * *

Within a fortnight they all converged on the marina in Battery Park. It was a beautiful day for sailing—winds north-northwest at ten to twelve knots, brilliant sunshine, and no appreciable waves yet on the Hudson.

"Hey, mate, good to meet you. Nattie here tells me you're a bobby dazzler. She's brought along some tucker and I've brought a pot of good cheer."

Natalia had prepped Jess with a few lessons in Australian. He took measure of Tom. He looked much more the seasoned Aussie skipper than an oily real estate mogul, with sun-baked skin, reddish-blond hair, and a habit of listing back and forth from port to starboard even before they got off dry land.

"*Bobby dazzler* means really cool and *tucker* means food," Natalia told Ethelinda. "I see you've brought some tucker too."

True to her mission, Ethelinda had lugged a basketful of German-Austrian sausage. "I've brought kasekrainer, bratwurst, weisswurst, mettwurst, und knackwurst. No better sausage."

The women hadn't coordinated. "Those look tasty," said Natalia, "but nothing holds a candle to kielbasa. I brought some. We'll have a friendly Austrian-Polish competition."

Peering through dreary thumb-worn magazines during downtime in the ER, Jess had read of Midwest family-reunion potlucks where every woman brought her best baked beans with sugar and bacon. There would be nothing else to eat, except maybe carrot Jell-O. These gatherings often didn't end well, either in the belly or interpersonal relations, and he was nervous about this sailing excursion. Friendly competition didn't look likely in light of how Austrians and Poles hit it off over the centuries.

They started upriver with Tom in the stern, Jess in the bow, and the two women under the boom tending the tucker. As they progressed, Tom filled the air with how to sail, and Natalia instructed Ethelinda on how not to cook. Jess found Tom's decibels all the more irritating because he had no interest in how to sail, and Ethelinda may have heard in Natalia's instruction a will-to-power over her own culinary know-how.

"Years since I've seen such a corker day for sailing, mate!" Tom shouted over the heads of the women. "Now I'm starboarding the helm . . . now I'm porting it." The *Spirit of Parmelia* zigzagged obediently as Jess tilted to the left and then to the right, grabbing the pulpit for balance. "Mind the jib up there, mate, we're going to tack to windward until we're wing and wing—you savvy?"

As they were passing Tribeca, where Robert De Niro had recently opened his Asian restaurant Nobu, Natalia launched a diatribe against fusion food. She had written many heated columns and was generally regarded as world leader of resistance to this faddish undoing of national identity, ethnic boundaries, culinary rules, and food authenticity. It wasn't clear that Ethelinda always knew what the famed restaurant reviewer was talking about.

"Why does Polish cuisine need anything from Asia?" Natalia said. "Buckwheat groats do well on their own, they don't need wasabi. Our cheesecake is no better with lemongrass. And does walrus sushi really improve with maple syrup? Do we really need to dunk abalone in cheese fondue? Is venison carpaccio any better soaked in soy sauce?"

"*Ja*, better soaked." Having been favored with ten minutes of culinary critique, Ethelinda was replying in a sullen monotone and nodding mechanically to everything Natalia said.

"Do we really need Lapsang tea–flavored beef with green miso or honey-roasted duck with coriander raita?"

"*Ja*, we really need them." Ethelinda grabbed at her knackwurst with a vengeance, yanking the segments apart for the grill.

"Austrian food may be more grub than cuisine, but at least it's authentic. It has a national identity. Agreed, Ethel?"

"*Ja*, national *identität*."

Tom continued his own irksome pedagogy. "Trim the sheets flat, mate . . . close-hauling this girl now, ease the tiller, spill the wind . . . aw, struth, there's a gale! Luffing now, never let a boat belly up."

The party reached a point about a hundred yards off the old Bank Street pier, and Tom dropped anchor for their picnic. He looked at the shoreline of the West Village and pointed out some houses on West Street that he had bought and sold, some of them to leather bars.

Jess stared at the waterfront and remembered what Natalia had told him of the Canarsee Indians, the sandy marshland, the trout streams and aromatic tobacco of the Sapokanican. But soon the natives were cast out of Eden by white traders. Their dubious dealings commenced the grand tradition of New World exploitation and commerce. He began dreaming his way into the past to escape this sailing party.

Natalia could often see a trance coming on just as people who live with diabetics learn to spot an insulin reaction. She pinched his upper arm and broke the spell. "Ouch!"

They gathered around the grill and began eating sausage and more sausage, then more sausage. Jess felt he shouldn't play favorites, so he accepted equal amounts of Austrian and Polish. Tom ate like a Great Barrier Reef sea cow while playing host. "Now will that be a middy or a schooner, me ladies?" That is, how large a glass of grog did they want? Natalia took a middy. Ethelinda, the first of many schooners. Each woman stuck to her own national sausages, passing them on to the menfolk with warm endorsements. Each glanced with disdain at the enemy sausage.

The competition over sausage didn't end in a food fight, and the party, stuffed, drunk, and flatulent, was ready to pull anchor and sail downriver. The wind seemed stronger, and clouds had darkened the sky.

"Mate, why don't you take a turn at the helm?"

"But I don't know anything about sailing."

"Not a problem. Just do what I tell you. Have a go at it."

Apprehensive but not knowing how to say no to the man whose domestic partner he was shtupping of a fashion, Jess took his place at the helm with Tom squeezed up behind him. He remembered sitting on the lap of one of his foster fathers at the wheel of a jeep—he was led to believe he was doing the driving, though his feet didn't reach the pedals. The garlic and cigar stench of that particular father made him carsick.

"Let's trim sail . . . Hold the winch there."

"Beg your pardon. Wench? Surely you don't mean Ethelinda." She had passed out by now in the hull.

"No, mate, that drum there—it helps you trim sail. And you gotta keep track of the tack, the luff, the leech, outhaul, backstay, jib, shrouds, the spreaders, and—what am I forgetting?—oh yeah, the boom, you gotta watch out for the boom if you've got a jibe on your hands, or you're dead in the water."

"Sounds like a lot to keep track of. But let's do it," said Jess gamely. He looked downriver at a large purple cloud that seemed to be coming their way. "Hmmm, the wind is picking up. Will that be a problem?"

"She'll be all right. This weather's a ripper for sailing. We're heading before the wind now. Let those sheets out, move the boom to a right angle. Let 'er go!"

Jess watched the cloud get larger and held on to the helm for dear life. Waves were increasing, and surely that was a squall coming their way. As it approached, Tom was shouting instructions into his ears that he was barely hearing. "Quick, give me that helm! Now, mate!"

Not budging, Jess was transported instead to a tall three-mast ship upon a painted river. On the shore, the early inhabitants of the island were harvesting maize and tobacco in harmony with a bountiful landscape. He waved to them his peaceful intentions, but they didn't see him. He tried to warn them not to buy those tchotchkes—then there never would be a Manhattan, a St. Vincent's Hospital, or even a Jess Freeman. But the scream stuck in his throat, just as his waving arm was suddenly inert, and everything in the panorama passed before his eyes in slow motion. The unfathomable guilt of the genocide was now his alone to bear.

It was then that the boom swung round and knocked him into the water. The life preserver knew which way was up, but Jess was bobbing down the main out of reach of the boat and taking water into his lungs.

He faintly heard Natalia telling Tom to please do something. He knew that without an intervention he'd be washed out to sea, passing by the Statue of Liberty to certain death. "Stone the crows!" cried Tom. He hopped to, put a lifeline around his waist, and leapt into the water. This left only Natalia to man the boat, and she knew little more about sailing than Jess. Tom shouted from the water as he swam doggedly toward Jess. "Ease the helm, toward the center, Nats, amidships!" Jess felt the strong arms of his rescuer around his chest and waist as Tom paddled back to the boat and pumped water from his lungs. He looked into Tom's face, relieved that mouth-to-mouth hadn't been necessary.

"No worries. You're safe now, mate."

"Ta Tom, ta a lot," said Jess, dredging up the Australian for thanks.

— Chapter Five —

THE MODERN PYGMALION

The next day Ethelinda dumped Jess because of the company he kept. She asked him to return all the frozen sausage, and that was that.

It can't be said that Jess's heart had been in this relationship or in the handful of non-Natalia liaisons over the next few months, then years. He narrated all of them in detail to Natalia. He found it odd that it was sexier to tell her these little stories than to experience them. Natalia listened and from time to time gave practical advice— like how to deal with temper tantrums inspired by calendar conflicts, and how to avoid paying for somebody's time-share in the Cayman Islands when he wasn't even being invited along.

He managed to stay out of the clutches of Tom, always in search of a good drinking companion. It was bad enough to feel unease over cuckolding the man who had saved his life. How could he become a drinking partner? But, um, it wasn't technically cuckolding since Natalia and Tom weren't married and, according to Natalia, Jess and she weren't even having sex.

Sometimes Jess imagined a man of demonic sexuality who would overpower her rules and withholding by sheer irresistibility. His name was Fergus. Natalia listened patiently to stories about Fergus. "He sounds enticing," she would say. "Yes, I'd let him do that." Sometimes she permitted mild phone sex, whether with Jess or Fergus, whom Jess would attempt to impersonate. But if he tried to change their actual bedroom protocol on every other Thursday, she would remind him what was permitted and what was not.

Jess began the move from Carmine to Bank Street the very day Mrs. Cimenti died. It was late February 1993 and the city was in a deep freeze. The other residents hoped the heirs in Naples would break with tradition and supply heat after 8:00 p.m. Later in the week, a mass was said at Our Lady of Pompeii on a Thursday afternoon. Natalia joined him at the cathedral and explained the ritual afterward because Jess's religious practice had never got beyond Native American animism. They made their way up Greenwich Avenue to the Bank Street townhouse. The movers had yet to show up with the furniture, including the cushions. Natalia and Jess went ahead and christened the new apartment, sitting in opposite corners on the chilly bedroom floor.

His practice was going well. He ceased making quick calls to his old mentors at Harvard to be reminded of the next step in a skin graft or eyelid lift. He was getting a handle on how to do them—he simply needed more practice. He tried to stay focused and guard against those sudden trances. His colleagues were okay with the two malpractice suits he brought upon them. In fact his reputation as "awesome" was established early on after he stitched up the mayor, involved in an early-morning barroom brawl near Jess's clinic, when a better plastic surgeon wasn't available.

The apartment at 23 Bank Street was a step up in status and elegance. Even though he got into the business with no thought of money, plastic surgeons cannot help getting rich. This was the fashionable West Village, full of landmark townhouses where the literati of earlier decades parked their rear ends, leaving historical markers. Jess bought the parlor apartment in a townhouse going co-op just a few doors from the long-demolished townhouse where Willa Cather had lived. Across the way was Charles Kuralt, then on his last leg in documenting back-roads American culture for CBS. Jess would see Bella Abzug's hat bouncing along outside his high parlor windows, not so swiftly as in earlier years because she too was about to be harvested by Old Father Time. And a few doors down stood the apartment building immortalized by the death of Sid Vicious of the Sex Pistols. "Sid Vicious died there! Sid Vicious died there!" chanted passersby.

Jess's living room had twelve-foot ceilings with ornate molding and built-in bookcases around an opulent fireplace of green marble from the Greek isle of Tinos. His back bedroom opened onto a courtyard, where the previous tenant had left a replica of Rodin's sculpture of Pygmalion and Galatea. Fully clothed, the sculptor was seated at Galatea's feet while she stood buck naked except for a coat of ice. He and Natalia weathered the winter and, with the advent of spring, looked forward to some quality post-fooling-around recovery time in the garden on late Thursday afternoons.

One such Thursday, shortly after noon, Jess was, as usual, seeing out-patients to gauge how their secondary infections were faring. He had Thursdays off after 3:00 p.m. and could look forward, every other week, to Natalia's visit. Before leaving his apartment he'd stashed a bottle of vintage Piper-Heidsieck and three ounces of Beluga, and he'd spit and polished Natalia's sex toys.

Just as he was telling his final patient to stay on the antibiotics and hope that removal of the chin implant wouldn't prove necessary, he had a call from the secretary that somebody had fallen from a horse in Central Park, suffering severe wounds to the face. Her neck and other vital parts were intact. She was being sped by medics to the clinic. Apparently aware of treatment rendered the mayor, the victim had put in an urgent request for Jess's services alone. Jess said he would wait long enough to inspect the injured party but could not sacrifice his Thursday afternoon. "Sounds as if she should find a better plastic surgeon, anyway," he muttered to the secretary.

She was a mess. Jess stared at abrasions, lacerations, hematomas, broken teeth, mangled ears, a broken nose, a possible orbital blowout fracture, deep scalp wounds, and marked facial asymmetry. He suppressed a *"Wow!"* and leaned over his patient, who was making small whimpering sounds and following him with her one still-open eye.

"Miss Epstein, can you tell me how this happened?"

She had also bitten her tongue but managed to speak through broken incisors, cracked bicuspids, and jaw dislocation. Jess leaned down and made out her words. "Docta Fweeman, I'm tho . . . gwateful."

"Miss Epstein, that's an unusual thing to hear at such a time. Patients usually complain. You fell off a horse? Weren't you wearing a helmet?"

While she tried to speak and Miss Prindle, the nurse, was setting up the I.V., he performed bimanual palpation—he felt her gently with both hands—to determine the extent of her injuries. The jaw clunked a little—yes, it was dislocated. "Sit up a minute, Miss Epstein. Very well, I'm applying traction to your mandibular condyle—" *Pop!* "There, it just slipped back into the glenoid fossa." Using technical vocabulary assured patients he knew the lay of the land. "Talking should be easier now."

"Yes, that helps. You're good at what you do. No, I'm embarrassed to say I wasn't wearing a helmet. But it wasn't my fault. It was the annual Spring Ride—Claremont sponsors it. Claremont Academy, that's where I work, I'm an equestrian."

This she said with obvious pride, which, like gratitude, was an emotion Jess didn't often register when dealing with patients extremely lacerated.

"We ride along the bridal path for half an hour, then we stop at Tavern on the Green for hot malt wine. It's a tradition. I organize it." As she spoke Jess was dabbing up blood with sterile gauze to get a better look at the damage. "We were sitting around the table making toasts . . . I'd just won first-in-show for equitation at the Annual Equestrian Competition at Madison Square Garden . . . and they were all toasting me . . . and every time, they toasted me I drank more wine. The rule is . . . don't drink and trot, or at least not too much. But do I ever follow the rules? . . . No, I never follow the rules."

"Oh."

"We were riding up the bridal path . . . then I galloped . . . it's against park regulations."

"Against regulations? Don't tell United Healthcare, Miss Epstein."

"It was great! We all tore out like Seabiscuit. Then I got this scary buzz in my right ear . . . It was some kind of hornet . . . and I ripped off the helmet . . . who wouldn't? But that upset my balance and my knees were weak from the wine, and I fell off Biskupski—he's my horse. Caught my left boot in the stirrup and couldn't release it . . . and Biskupski went into a panic and kept galloping for all he was worth, and this set off a stampede of the other horses . . . and he dragged me along the cinder path and then veered off. My head was hitting against everything along the way, I couldn't tell what all. Maybe for half a minute . . . it seemed forever. Then he veered back to the path in front of the stampeding horses and my foot got free just in time to get trampled to death."

"Trampled? You do look a little the worse for wear but not quite dead. The medics said you have just a few bruises below the neck. I'll check you out all over in just a minute."

"Before I passed out, I saw all these thundering horses coming at me. They must have mistaken me for a log in a steeplechase, because they leapt over. I took just a few glancing hoofs to the head . . . You see, that's one reason I'm grateful—I'm not dead yet. The other's that I'm in your hands, doctor. I know how good you are—and kind."

"Kind? I'm just a professional doing my job. I took the oath by what's his name."

"I saw the interview on NY1 after the mayor's brawl. You were kind enough to do a good job on that thug even though you deplore his politics."

"Miss Epstein, how do you know anything about my politics?"

Pause. "It's just an instinct I have—I'm sure you deplore his politics."

"Well, I may be kind sometimes, but after this evaluation I'll bring in another plastic surgeon. I've got a pressing engagement this afternoon. Sorry."

Long pause. Then her body trembled and she began hyperventilating. Her open eye stared up at him, so dark brown it was almost black and unusually large—the eye gleamed with mesmeric force. Then, from her deepest gut, "But, please, please, you have to help me!"

"I'm sorry, I can't just duck out of other responsibilities. And frankly I'm a little out of my depth with your injuries."

"No, you must help me! *You must!*" He turned away, shaken by her plea, and without reflection, said, "Okay, Miss Epstein. I'll do it, all right already. But don't expect a miracle. There are limits to what a plastic surgeon can do. You're going to need lots of work."

"You're awesome, doctor. I *knew* you'd take me... I'm so grateful. You've made my day."

"Okay, Miss Epstein, that's enough. We'll get to work right away. But I must make a brief phone call."

Jess left the room. He didn't know what to say to Natalia. He had never broken an engagement with her and couldn't fully explain even to himself why he'd given in to this patient. It wasn't exactly pity—it was, well, odd.

"Nattie! Jess here... Uh, this is terrible but I'm forced to cancel. A patient's just come in, a god-awful emergency. It's hard to make out her face, such a mess. Up to me to salvage her. It's going to take maybe ten hours for just the preliminaries."

Silence. Jess squirmed.

"You told me you're not even very good at plastic surgery," Natalia then said. "What do you mean, it's up to you? There's Dr. De Zwirek and Dr. Ditkoff, and there's Dr. Dermksian."

"They're all booked." Jess rarely lied.

"You were booked, Jess. What am I, chopped ham hock?"

"Nattie, please... I'll make it up to you."

"You can try. Call me sometime, mister."

She hung up. He felt like a serpent shut out of paradise. But he took heart that at least she wasn't totally casual about their dates. And this surprised him a little.

Well, maybe keeping dates was just one rule among others. Or could she be jealous? That would be asking too much.

He returned to the examination room. "Okay, Miss Epstein, we're going to prep you for some procedures—but this will be no walk in the park—sorry—not easy sailing. By the end of the day we'll have you all stitched up. I'm afraid there may be some fractures. C-T scans, MRIs, and x-rays will tell the tale. Can't do this all by myself. We need an oral and maxillofacial surgeon—Dr. Levy will have a better idea about those bones and teeth. Now just lie back and relax, and leave the stitching to me."

"Doctor, I hope I haven't interfered with any plans."

"The patient always comes first."

"You said you'd check me all over."

"Uh, thanks for the reminder, Nattie . . . I mean Miss Epstein."

"Nattie . . . Nattie . . . I've always liked that name. Go ahead, call me Nattie. Call me anything you like."

Jess found it remarkable that Miss Epstein complained so little that first day, thinking she must have emotional reserves more ample than his other patients, some of whom made a bigger fuss about a pimple than she made about messing up a fair amount of her face. What could account for this?

With Nurse Prindle's assistance, the body check revealed nothing more than a few scrapes and bruises, and no more broken bones. It revealed something else—a well-honed body, more muscular than Natalia's, with a gold ring perforating her left nipple and a black spider tattoo just above her pubis. As a facial plastic surgeon Jess didn't ordinarily see his patients in the buff, and he now doubted his professionalism—this felt more like the male gaze than disinterested medical observation.

"Do you have a recent photograph? It's a big help if we know what you're supposed to look like." He paused and thought maybe that was an awkward way of putting it.

"No, doctor. Anyway, I . . . I don't like the way I'm supposed to look."

So Jess started from scratch, quite determined to do a good job on this patient, who presented the biggest challenge yet to his craft. Maybe this was his own rite of passage, and on the other end he would be a truly awesome plastic surgeon, a fake no longer. Sure, there were some procedures he needed to pick up along the way. But for now it was simply a matter of suturing the lacerations with number six thread and doing some routine flaps and skin grafts. Maybe Nurse Prindle would stop berating him as if he were an apprentice seamstress.

The suturing went well into the evening. As it turned out, the lacerations weren't very deep, which boded well for healing. But Dr. Levy arrived and confirmed a few broken facial bones, including a nasal fracture, a zygomatic arch or cheekbone fracture, and maxilla—or midface—fractures that bent and elongated an already long face. Fortunately, an orbital blowout of the right eye was ruled out—she had only a black eye or, more loftily put, ecchymosis and periorbital edema.

So began a one-year romp of extreme plastic surgery. During this time Jess knew better than to schedule Miss Epstein for a Thursday afternoon. Natalia canceled one Thursday rendezvous two weeks following his own cancellation, and Jess felt this was fair retaliation. But then she seemed to forget the slight, and their biweekly sessions resumed with no change of protocol and no questions asked about Miss Epstein. Natalia was one structure in his personal life that seemed durable even if it didn't offer Nirvana to either party.

* * *

Rhinoplasty was first on the plate after the initial suturing, the sooner the better because Miss Epstein's nose was smushed. "Okay, what kind of nose did you have?"

"A Jewish nose. *Epstein*, you know—for Christ's sake. Please don't restore my Jewish nose. Give me an Irish nose."

"If you say so, but Irish noses went out in the late fifties. What about a fusion nose—you know, the best of both? The fusion nose is cutting edge, my specialty."

"Just give me the nose *you'd* like to see on a woman."

There were some details to be worked out first, such as whether to harvest fresh cartilage and bone from a rib or go with Gore-Tex. The standard use of ear cartilage was ruled out because her ears were pretty much demolished and in need of radical otoplasty somewhere down the road.

"From my rib? Who do you think you are—Yahweh? And isn't it supposed to be the other way around? You're Adam, the rib comes from you."

"Okay, very funny, but the real issue is pleural leakage—you know, whether or not I'll puncture a lung."

They went with Gore-Tex. "We call this camouflaging—we put the implant material into the deformity. It gives the impression of a real nose."

"You mean I'm going to end up with a fake nose?"

"Miss Epstein, you're going to end up with a fake face."

And so the procedures were underway. The rhinoplasty turned out better than Jess could have imagined. Admittedly, he had scratched his head while stenting a sandwich graft in the submucoperichondrial plane, and he was forced to revisit the geometry of the Simons tip. After that, it was easy sailing. When the bandages came off, there stood the fusion nose—part Irish and part Jewish yes, but he threw in just a dash of Estonian. "It's a little big now, Miss Epstein. That's just the swelling. When it subsides you'll have a much-sought-after nose."

As the weeks and months progressed she reported for procedure after procedure. Next up was her chin. "I had a weak chin for such a long face." And a bit of her weak chin had itself been scraped off. Now she wanted a chin like Joan Crawford's. So after studying photos of the movie star, Jess elected Teflon as the implant material, shaped it as best he could along the lines of *Mommie Dearest* but threw in some Faye Dunaway, factored in Merrifield's Z-angle, made an incision under what remained of the jaw, tucked in the Teflon, did a skin graft, and stitched her up. The result was once again beyond what Jess could have hoped for—it suggested fortitude, of course, but it was also a little scary, this new chin.

"I never liked my old cheekbones," she told Jess as they next prepared for malar implantation. "Not high enough. What can you do for me?" This wouldn't be a mere vanity exercise because those glancing horse hoofs had created concavities where there should have been protuberances—better put, malar hypoplasia and facial asymmetry. Jess had brushed up on Gonzalez-Ulloa's and Hinderer's work on malar augmentation. Miss Epstein was an ideal candidate because of her long, narrow face. "Think I'll be using polyethylene this time, Miss Epstein, unless you'd prefer polymethylmethacrylate."

"Polyethylene—you mean the stuff they use on floors?"

"More or less. Don't worry, you're not parquet. I'll throw in a lower-lid blepharoplasty at the same time."

"I beg your pardon?"

"Eyelid surgery. The two procedures together will create a powerful synergy between your cheekbones and eyes, not unlike the Mona Lisa."

The effect was stunning. Only a few procedures remained— otoplasty ("my old ears stuck out, doctor, please improve on them"), dental implants ("I used to have a large space between my front teeth—can you improve on that?"), upper-lip augmentation with Brigitte Bardot as the model, and finally dermal abrasion to smooth out any evidence of scarring. Dr. Levy corrected the elongation of face that resulted from the maxilla fracture and somehow managed to shorten the face even more. Though he was a physician whose credentials far outweighed Jess's, Dr. Levy didn't reap anything like the same adulation.

As the months wore on and Margaret Epstein's face shaped up, an intimacy was springing up between Jess and his patient. They shared the larger contours of their life stories. Margaret told him of how she came from Jewish aristocracy in Miami, where her father owned a franchise of restaurants and her mother a high-end boutique of accessories. And how she'd been sent to the finest schools, beginning with a prestigious Hebrew nursery, moving on to Jacobson Sinai Academy, and ending up at Smith, where she had a private suite within the elite dormitory. She decorated it with equestrian trophies and was excused from class whenever an important competition was at hand. Majoring in art history, she made her grades but was an indifferent student. Her passion wasn't for art but for horses, despite the taunts she got for her long face. "Would you call Maggie's love of horses narcissistic?" one of her smart-ass Smith peers asked the instructor in a psych class—and everyone laughed while she held her hands to inflamed cheeks. But she had the last laugh because she was loaded, now living at The Pierre hotel on Fifth Avenue and working at Claremont just for the fun of it.

She confessed to Jess, when out of earshot of Nurse Prindle, that her love of horses was erotic. This was a stereotype that young female equestrians often confronted—and in her case it was true. She had fallen in love with horse after horse, especially stallions but she had crushes on geldings and fillies as well. She loved to ride bareback in her youth and felt with explosive pleasure the relentless movement of back, loin, and croup. The horse's chest, shoulder, and quarters radiated up into her own muscles as she pressed her knees against the steamy flank—or words to that effect. She whispered to Jess that she had her first orgasm riding bareback at thirteen, not knowing then what it was, as she cantered an Andalusian filly named Esmeralda. It had been against regulations to ride bareback and she was chastised by the stable keeper. This made her wish to repeat the wrong. She would sneak Esmeralda onto a neighboring field in moonlight, out of earshot of the stable keeper. Sometimes she would take the stallion, Señor Fernandez. She sensed the horses knew what she was up to as she pressed against their undulating backs. They let her, they liked it. It was cantering that worked best, so she paid short shrift to walking, trotting, and galloping.

Trading down from naked horse flesh to English saddle, she rapidly learned dressage, cross-country, show jumping, and even steeplechasing, winning her division as a teenager in the three-day Rolex Grand Slam Eventing. She loved hot-blooded Arabians, both stallions and fillies, and enjoyed mastering such animals to the enhancement of her trophy case. And she had developed a taste for the wild Polish horse, the Konik, a modern breed that recaptures equine primitivism. She personally tamed three Koniks at Claremont.

Jess affected indifference to these stories, telling Miss Epstein to refrain from speaking whenever a subtle procedure was underway and Nurse Prindle was present. Surely he shouldn't seriously register any of her personal mutterings but simply go about his craft. But she was getting under his skin.

"Won't you be nervous about getting back on a horse, any horse, say a palfrey, let alone a wild horse?" Jess was worried that all his stitching would be for nothing if she once again presented with a bloody stump of a head. Two blepharoplasties were enough.

"No. Whatever happens I can't wait to get back in the saddle."

Margaret would talk horses as Jess prepped her for the various procedures, and sometimes, just as she was coming out of anesthesia, she would mutter things that offered a window into her naked id. It seemed a violation of her privacy, but his ears could not choose but hear, though he didn't always grasp what the id was talking about. "Bring the teaser over . . . that's right, now he's ready . . . good going, Przewalski . . . Sit in front of me, yes, I'll teach you . . . Let's go into this booth . . . You like that transvestite singing Sinatra, don't you? I can tell . . . All right girl, let's canter!" And she would have an unmistakable orgasm right there in his office.

Physicians are taught to expect this as an occasional consequence of a large dose of nitrous oxide, more common in female than male patients. Nurse Prindle would look embarrassed on Margaret's behalf. Of course they never told her afterward. He figured that patients have worse ways of dealing with surgery.

He then found himself telling her bits and pieces of his own life—the foster parents, growing up in the Southwest, his adjustment to the Big Apple. No, he preferred not to discuss the enigma of his biological parents. Then one day when she had come to and Nurse Prindle wasn't present, she asked, "And what about romance? You've never mentioned a wife. Do you have girlfriends?"

"I've placed a few personals in *The New York Review of Books* but never mention that I'm a plastic surgeon. They find that out on our first date."

"How do you describe yourself?"

"Something like this—*Dear You, I'm not lots of fun. I hate long walks on the beach and all popular music. My looks are so-so, and I'm only five-eight but even-tempered with clean fingernails. They called me 'carrot top' as a kid but my hair is now dull brown and thinning. I have green eyes—I know, hazel is better in a man. And I'm indifferent in the sack. I already have a girlfriend but am allowed to see her only once every two weeks. This leaves plenty of time for you, if you're willing to explore options. Please no photo, just a sample of your handwriting. Pygmalion.* Spoofing about some of this, Miss Epstein, but whatever ad I place, I get lots of responses. Can women be this hard up?"

"I'd respond. But you say you already have a girlfriend?"

"Her name's Nattie. You once said you like that name."

"It has some associations . . . Don't let me pry, but"—Margaret leaned forward—"what's her appeal?"

"We both like chili. What more can I tell you?"

"Lots more, whenever you like, doctor. By the way, why don't you call me Maggie?"

"Maggie? Okay, Miss Epstein."

"And may I call you Jess? I know that's forward but I'm getting a new face. Get ready, I'm going to answer your ad!"

After the Ethelinda fiasco, Jess was wary, but there was something contagious in Miss Epstein's passion for horses. Though he was no stallion, he began fantasizing about her riding on *his* back, grabbing his mane, and holding on for dear life as he neighed and cantered.

He would be seeing her in a month for a final evaluation after the dermal abrasion and sundry swellings had simmered down. But a few days later, he received a handwritten response to the personal ad he'd embellished for her amusement.

My dear Pygmalion, I'm answering your ad with caution. I fear that you are a creep. Clean fingernails—are you by chance a plastic surgeon? You couldn't be a sculptor. I like it that you are indifferent in the sack—leave that to me, I'm an enthusiast. Also a world-class equestrian, eager to take you riding. Galatea.

She began making frequent appearances in his dreams, sometimes as a bloody stump but more often as a work of art, radiant in her symmetry, honed features, and probing brown-black eyes. Once she appeared as an Andalusian filly and he mounted her, throwing his hoofs over her croup and throbbing his way to the stars in a Lexington mating stable.

This was a highly unprofessional dream.

The day came for the unveiling. A year had passed since her accident in 1993. He'd not seen her for a month because there was no more work for him to do, and it was now simply a matter of letting her face heal on its own. It was early spring again and not a Thursday. The city was awash in flowering trees as he whistled his way down Bank Street to the Hudson Street clinic. Her appointment was at 3:00 p.m., so he had plenty of time to make mistakes on other patients in the meantime. He was preoccupied. "No, doctor, it's the left ear, *the left!*"

What would she look like now? She had been a piece of pulp, and he had relied on all his artifice to fabricate a new face. Also on some hunches that seemed to come out of nowhere, a kind of primordial instinct guiding his scalpel. Plastic surgery has its limits. Patients must be told not to expect too much, no silk purse out of a sow's ear. But as Jess had worked away, he'd felt as if he were overcoming those limits, as if some enigmatic force, both without and within, were empowering his craft.

The secretary announced the arrival of Miss Epstein, and Jess told Nurse Prindle that he could handle this one on his own and she should prep the next patient. A brisk knock and there she stood, coyly holding a large sun hat over her face. She came in. He found himself locking the door and hoping the nurse wouldn't hear the click.

"Hello, Jess. How do you like my costume?" She was wearing a gauzy blouse that didn't quite conceal the nipple ring he knew lurked beneath. A slip was masquerading as a skirt, and he could see the curves of her derriere that made it obvious she was wearing a thong. Some hair transplants to cover bald spots had taken hold, and her long smooth hair had been recently transformed by a beautician from mousy brown to lustrous red—the color he told her he preferred.

"You are dressed beautifully, Miss Epstein, er Maggie. But when are you going to show me your face? Let's see your face!"

"Have a look, Pygmalion. It's *your* face, you made it." She slowly raised the hat and revealed a face that rivaled your routine Greek goddess in exquisite contours and pale marbling. Jess tried to suspend disbelief at what he himself had wrought.

"Miss Epstein! You *are* Galatea!"

"So would you like to kiss the face you made, doctor?"

He shuddered as they lay back on the examination table. They touched tongues and, except for his white doctor's robe, didn't take time to undress. He pushed up her blouse and kissed her nipples, catching an incisor briefly on the ring but managing to unbuckle as she raised her skirt and pushed her thong down as far as her knees. Then she turned over.

"Do it horsy, doctor, horsy. Would Nattie do this? Would she?"

Jess politely mounted from behind with no condom. So much for safe sex with a doctor. She neighed only once before he came, in maybe twenty seconds.

"You're quick in the saddle, doctor."

"Miss Epstein," he gasped. "Your appointment lasts an hour. Give me some recovery time. Let's try it again."

They were just resuming when Nurse Prindle knocked and rattled the doorknob. "Doctor Freeman! What's going on in there? Are you dead?"

"Alive and well, Miss Prindle. That was some racket from next door. Tell my five o'clock I'll be with him shortly."

"Let's pretend we're in a stable," Margaret whispered. "We'll do it nice and slow so we don't disturb the horses in the next stall. They'd get antsy."

He was feeling his oats, and though he doubted she came, he was elated at entering a dreamworld he himself had fashioned, awakening to find this dream was real.

Chapter Six

THE PROMISE

Jess broke with custom and didn't tell Natalia about his new relationship for many weeks. When he was constrained to fess up, he didn't mention the circumstances of their meeting and the plastic surgery. They simply met through personals, he said. He had to say this much because the affair was outed by the press and Natalia came across a photograph of the two in the *Times* society pages, not far removed from her pan of a new restaurant, Babbo, which specialized in baked testicles.

How the photo got there was predictable in hindsight. Jess and Margaret began seeing each other frequently after that impassioned moment on the examination table. Except she was no longer Margaret Epstein. She changed her legal name to Gilah de Champigny, explaining to Jess that she was entitled to the elegant surname through her maternal line, extending back to French Jewish aristocracy in the sixteenth century.

Never knowing what to do with all his money, Jess bought a tux and began accepting invitations to benefits. He invited Gilah along on many of these. When asked about herself at the $5,000-donor tables, Gilah would speak of her string of polo ponies in Argentina, her stud farm in Ireland, and her Kentucky thoroughbreds, many with Native Dancer in their bloodlines. She was a strong advocate of keeping thoroughbred lines free of artificial insemination. These exquisite equines must be conceived the old-fashioned way. She was heated on the subject.

Jess listened with some puzzlement to all the stretchers when she spoke to rich people and society columnists.

"A string of polo ponies goes well with my new face," she explained to him later. "And aren't we all supposed to be re-inventing ourselves? Look, I'm plenty rich, just not *that* rich."

Re-inventing was then a fairly new cliché.

Meanwhile, the press, from the *Times* to *Newsday* to *People* to the *Star*, was milking this new glamorous couple.

AWESOME PLASTIC SURGEON SEEN AT 21 WITH RICH
BEAUTY CHICK!
ARE MOVIES IN THE CARDS FOR GLAM GILAH?
PAPARAZZI ELUDED BY SEXY CELEBS ON HORSEBACK!

Jess had so outdone himself that nobody guessed Gilah's face was the product of plastic surgery. With her new fame, Gilah could hardly return to Claremont Riding Academy except in the role of new patron and occasional rider. She wasn't recognized, and she would often hear employees speak of her in not very flattering terms—"Old horsy-face" or "Things sure are better here without that big bosser, still I kinda miss her." Gilah was no longer merely an accomplished equestrian. As a rare beauty she was exempted from doing anything. She continued living at The Pierre. Oddly, she never invited Jess up whenever he dropped her off after one of their forays.

So that she might live the rich life at a still higher pitch, she decided to get richer, asking Jess if he would invest in a new unisex cosmetic line, to be incorporated as House of Gilah de Champigny and copyrighting such brand names as Gilah's Filly Cream, Gilah's Teaser Lotion, and Gilah's Trifecta Rinse. This would be doing something without exactly sinking to "trade." Jess said yes but, knowing little about money, consulted with Tom, who had the entrepreneurial track record. This meant drinks at the White Horse Tavern.

"Let's park our bums over in that corner, mate, and get us some schooners. Nattie says you guys are ant's pants these days. I don't read the papers. You got some bizo for me?"

Over fish and chips, Jess explained that it was actually Gilah's business. Did he have any advice and, incidentally, would he like to invest? He silently thought that if Gilah turned a profit, it would be compensation to Tom for his accessing Natalia every two weeks, easing some conscience in the matter. But Tom said he didn't wish to put his money on Drongo.

"Drongo?"

"Yeah, the only horse in Australia that never won a race. But I'll give it some thought, mate."

A few days later Tom came through with quite a bit of advice on shady dealing and how to turn a profit. He also put up one hundred thousand as venture capital with the understanding that one product would be called Gilah's Billabong Conditioner. Jess was grateful but wondered, as usual, what Natalia saw in Tom. Successful in her own right, she didn't need a sugar daddy.

Natalia was nonplussed when she saw the first photos of the new socialites. "Why didn't you tell me about her right away like all the others? What's different about Gilah? What's she got that Ethelinda didn't?"

Jess hesitated, thinking there was one plain difference. Gilah was the new look for the nineties, and the look didn't resemble weisswurst.

But there was a deeper motive for his reticence. Used to maintaining a certain distance from women even in the midst of infatuation—a distance that was one source of compatibility with Natalia, who outdid him in distance—he now hungered for greater intimacy with Gilah. He felt some entitlement. Having fashioned a new surface for this spirited equestrian, he wished to explore the interior.

"I don't know, Nattie. I just didn't get around to it. She doesn't hold a candle to you, believe me." Yes, he was becoming adept at lying. Uncorking the champagne and lighting the candles, he set out the usual choice edibles next to the bed, including kielbasa.

"Do you always remember to clean up this joint for our Thursdays? Gilah looks fairly clean in those photos, but I'd appreciate some Clorox."

"I'm religious about it. And yeah, she's very clean."

But Jess was in a state of identity conflation. Whenever he had oppositional sex with Natalia, the image of Gilah intruded, and whenever he had up-close sex with Gilah, the image of Natalia intruded. He wondered what images intruded in *their* minds, in keeping with Freud's familiar observation that two people are never alone in bed.

Jess was flattered by the hint of possessiveness in Natalia. But he was puzzled by Gilah, who was oddly insistent that Jess keep his Thursday appointments. And she was always asking for details of their lovemaking, despite its repetitiveness. When she began asking for details at the very moment they were playing horsy, Jess heard what images were intruding.

"Was she wearing those frumpy white undies again? Did you fizz champagne all over her like last time? Did she say things from her corner? . . . Well, what did she say?"

Gilah was always eager to hear everything, and Jess slowly caught on that she was especially tempestuous in her lovemaking on Fridays. *Hmmm, maybe Gilah was bi.*

When they weren't in bed, they did the town and continued to be followed by press and celebrity hounds. Gilah gave him riding lessons in Central Park. He managed to stay on his horse, which, he couldn't help but reflect, was doing Gilah herself one better. Common folk would wave upon recognizing them, and sometimes they were pursued by other riders who copied their gaits and gratefully ate dust. Gilah was often asked to autograph celebrity photos. Like most celebrities, she was famous for being famous. Jess was hounded also, if not to the same degree. He was famous for a reason—his plastic surgery on the mayor—but this didn't have the same clout as being famous for no reason at all.

All these attentions—from the press and from these two capable women—were going to Jess's head. If only Alison of Santa Fe could see him now! His irritating habit of ironic self-deprecation had been grounded in an honest estimate of his limitations. If he were the first to admit of these, he could duck the judgmental gaze of others. Such was his motive. But maybe he had been underestimating himself all along. Maybe he was a star, both in his field and in bed.

The emergence of vanity in this humble fellow was betrayed in behavioral changes. He started whistling. He hired a cleaning lady and a publicist. He decided he was entitled to more than one pair of wearable shoes at a time. He began a diary—his was now a life worth recording. Worse, he briefly visited a psychoanalyst. Only a mental health professional could have failed to see that Jess was entering a manic state of mind feeding off Gilah, as the two watched their grandiose reflections in the public imagination.

A year passed with little incident other than a compounding of his and her fame, and the launch of Gilah's line of beauty products. Natalia and Jess's bi-Thursdays continued with little variation in protocol.

The second weekend in October 1995, Jess hired a driver and off they sped in a Mercedes to Mohonk Mountain House near New Paltz in the Shawangunk Mountains, the Gunks. It was peak season for foliage and would be a perfect weekend to sample the eighty-five miles of bridle paths and hiking trails. They checked into a pentagonal room in one of the turrets of the huge Victorian mansion-hotel. The owners were Quakers who outlawed drinking, smoking, gaming, and dancing. Natalia had panned their kitchen in an unkind column on resort cooking. This left sex the only kinetic pleasure open to visitors, mostly geriatrics who spent the day in porch rockers waiting for dinner.

Gilah and Jess were given two sway-backed nags at the stable and told to walk them slowly wherever they liked. But the landscape was ample compensation. The central ridge of quartz, sandstone, and shale was an imposing structure, a northern extension of the Appalachians reaching above two thousand feet—the Hard Rock Café of rock climbers. On the ridge grew hemlocks, chestnut oaks, and dwarf pines. They passed peat and cedar swamps, stream bogs, waterfalls and mountain lakes of unusual depth. And here and there the sprinkling of gazebos reminded Nature that she exists only to be viewed by humans.

"If this terrain were a face, it'd need dermal abrasion," said Jess, trying to be clever. "The last Ice Age did little to smooth out the ridges and fissures." He was following Gilah down a steep talus slope and hoping his nag wouldn't suffer a coronary.

"Dermal abrasion . . . Jess, have you ever mentioned my surgeries to Nattie?"

"Of course not. Why should she know? The only people who know are Dr. Levy and Miss Prindle and, yeah, thousands of people working for United Healthcare. Your secret is safe with me."

"Let's park our nags here," she said when they had safely reached the borders of a red maple swamp. "Jess, this place is making me horny."

"Must be the place—your nag can't canter."

"Is Mohonk for lovers?" she asked, placing a plastic, flannel-backed tablecloth over the damp leaves.

"You've heard about those orgies in nursing homes. The fire doesn't always go out after seventy-five. Some of my clients hope to shave three decades off their façades because they want more action."

The sunlight reflected off Gilah's shimmering red hair and brought out the stunning contours of her fake face. As they sank into turkey-and-iceberg-lettuce sandwiches and swilled down malt wine, they stared at the uplifted folds and fissures and the deep crevasse where they had made their way. This dramatic landscape somehow put Jess in mind of Natalia's ample body.

"Why don't you introduce me to Nattie sometime, Jess? I feel I already know her, inside and out."

Jess tended to keep his people categories distinct. He gave no parties and introduced nobody to anybody. "If you know her, Gilah, why do you need to meet her?"

"There's always more to a person than what people say. And maybe she'd like to meet *me*."

"Oh, I don't think so. I'm not sure you'd get along. Why take a chance?"

"I take chances, Jess. Are you some kind of chickenshit? Come on, take a chance. Introduce us."

"I think she wants me all to herself on Thursdays."

"So presumptuous! Anyway, I didn't say I'd horn in on you two. Just introduce us, Jess."

They continued sipping wine. The sun was getting low and it was chilly. Gilah knelt behind him and began rubbing his shoulders. "You feel tense, love. What's there to worry about way out here? Nobody's around, want to snuggle?"

"Right here in the open?"

"Why not? Miss Prindle isn't listening in."

She caressed him from behind then pulled him onto his back. "Yes, you're ready! Let's do it." She pulled off her slacks and straddled him.

"Okay, Nattie, do it."

"Nattie? Fine, I'll be Nattie for you."

"Oh . . . sorry about that, Gilah. You're Gilah. Too much wine."

"Introduce me to Nattie," she said, suspending her body over his. "Promise, you schnook!"

"No, I won't. Just sit down, please, just a little bit, pretty please."

"I can perch here forever. Introduce me to Nattie. Promise?"

She gave a little and withdrew. He had no choice. "All right, Nattie, I mean Gilah, I promise."

"The Thursday after next. It's Halloween. We all go to the parade in costume. Promise!"

"I promise. Just do it!"

She did. He finished in the usual twenty seconds. Gilah didn't object. She was smiling, her dental implants glowing. Jess, meanwhile, was drifting into a trance.

Natalia, Gilah, and he were foot-high Czech puppets performing at La Mama before a vaguely hostile audience already wanting its money back. He tried to look up to see who was pulling their strings as they danced a peasant dance set to Dvorak. The puppeteers were nowhere to be seen above the proscenium. He felt like a klutz next to the two spirited women, who swirled gracefully and looked behind to see if he could mimic their steps. He tried to do better but wondered what the plot was.

He came out of his trance as they got back on the wretched nags. He looked up the darkening crevasse and its walls were closing in on him.

— *Chapter Seven* —

PARADE'S END

"Good to meet you at last, Nattie. Jess has told me all about you!"

"Yes, Gilah, Jess has told me all about you too," Natalia replied archly. "I try to avoid the society pages."

Nervous laughter from Jess, who thought maybe he should place himself 'twixt these mighty opposites and keep the conversation on matters of little import.

They all met at the annual Halloween parade through the West Village. Jess went as Jack Kevorkian, with a scythe and a compact suicide kit strapped to his back. He asked for volunteers among the onlookers who lined the streets. Natalia went as Julia Child, with a breadbasket full of leaflets describing how to make blood pudding in thirty-nine easy steps. Dressed frumpily, she carried extra padding except where she didn't need any, and took wheezy deep breaths. Gilah went as herself, with a black-and-white photograph of her new face enlarged and propped in front. The effect was uncanny. Dressed to kill in a tight sequined party dress from Bergdorf's, she carried a cornucopia of samples from the Champigny line of beauty products to distribute along the way.

Jess could take credit for most everything, constructing the Kevorkian and Child masks overnight and having made Gilah's mask the hard way over an entire year.

They noticed right away that many revelers were wearing rubber masks of Gilah de Champigny. There were almost as many Gilahs as there were Madonnas.

Jess was relieved when Natalia assumed her role as tour guide. "Did you know this parade was quite different just a decade ago, Gilah? It wound through old narrow streets of the West Village like a serpent, and onlookers were genuine Villagers. It was a real celebration of the dead. Now it's become a big tourist attraction on boring Sixth Ave. The onlookers are losers from Jersey and the Bronx."

Gilah cringed. "The Bronx, yuk!"

The parade was forming at Sixth Avenue and Spring Street, with giant puppet skeletons slowly leading the way, each propped up on long sticks by marchers. Other puppets and macabre figures on stilts from the Bread & Puppet Theater joined the death parade. Near the front, Jess looked back and saw the thick band of twenty thousand marchers extending downtown, framed by the Twin Towers, always lit up at night by row after row of windows as janitors emptied paper shredders and replenished water coolers. He was struck by the immense incongruities of life—unwavering steel girders versus pliable papier-mâché, irrepressible carnality versus death inevitable.

"Another difference is there aren't so many gays and transvestites," said Natalia.

"Because they're dead?" asked Gilah.

"Dead or siphoned off by the Pride Parade and Wigstock," Natalia said, alluding to the festival of transvestites wearing foot-high wigs that was held in Tompkins Square Park every August.

"I used to wear wigs," said Gilah, "then I settled for my own hair. It just needed a little highlighting. Now I've got my own conditioner, your guy named it Gilah's Billabong . . . Say, where's Tom? I owe him a lot—was hoping to meet him at long last." This was disingenuous. Jess had already told Gilah they'd be spared Tom tonight.

"He's sailing off the coast of New Zealand looking for pirate booty. It's one of his hobbies." Natalia tossed some leaflets as she strode along and scrutinized her fellow marchers. "It's a shame about the gays and HIV. Lesbians have managed to stay negative, but I don't see many of them either."

Jess thought she underestimated the sexual fringe. He saw transvestites with naked plastic boobs and a lady cop wearing a thong on her huge rubber butt. A nun lifted her habit and flashed a dildo just as they were passing Our Lady of Pompeii at Father Demo Square.

Natalia took this sacrilege in stride and continued her lecture. "The Celts get some credit for Halloween. They got things started with the festival of Samhain, the end of summer. Their Druids communed with the dead and found out what lay in store for the tribe—you know, famine and disease and bad weather. But it's the Catholic Church that deserves most of the credit."

"Nattie has a bias."

"Let her talk, Jess. I love to listen to you talk, Nattie." Gilah pushed Jess aside and sidled up to Natalia.

"It's left over from my lecture-tour days," said Natalia. "Also maybe a bit of catechism training. So anyway, the Catholics didn't just banish pagan festivals, they turned Samhain into All Saints' Day. Good old Pope Boniface the Fourth . . ."

"Doesn't he turn up somewhere in Dante's *Inferno*?" asked Gilah, hoping, maybe, to flout her academic pedigree.

"That was the bad Boniface—the Eighth. He killed six thousand people in the village of Palestrina and ended up in the eighth circle where he belongs. The good Boniface told his flock to go parade their saints' relics through the villages and put on costumes to honor them. Those old shins and knuckles would scare off evil spirits. The night before All Saints' Day was All Hallows' Eve, and that got shortened to Halloween—and it's devolved now into a parade where a nun salutes the church with a dildo." She winced.

"That would scare me off," said Gilah, casting samples of Teaser Lotion and Filly Cream to admirers behind the police barricades. "Where do Jews fit into all this? I'm Jewish, you know."

"Jews were bogeymen—their features got parodied—Gilah, you've totally escaped the stereotype—and, uh, their effigies would be ritually burned at the stake. Halloween's a great time for burning scapegoats."

"Make it up by being nice to me, Nattie. We could do our own little thing—you teach me Latin and I teach you Hebrew . . . Don't laugh, I'm serious!"

They passed the old Jefferson Market Library with the giant spider that every year climbs slowly down the turret. Jess thought of Gilah's pubic tattoo.

She continued, "I do know some Polish," and she proved it by singing "I Want to Hold Your Hand" in Polish. "I know more than that. I've been studying it on and off now for years."

"But why?" Natalia asked.

"I used to be a loner—didn't want to do what everybody else was doing. I eat Polish food too, on the side, not with Jess. He says he gets more than enough Polish food when he gets together with you on your Thursdays."

"So Jess, have you been laying in all that kielbasa just to humor me? Hypocrite!" She thrust her recipe for blood pudding in his hands. "Next Thursday this is what I want, no kielbasa. All thirty-nine steps, no cheating."

They passed the New School for Social Research on their right at Thirteenth Street. "I even took some courses on Central European history and culture over there," Gilah said, "while everybody else was studying Western Europe. Western Europe is passé . . . I studied Polish, Czech, and Romanian history just for fun."

"Romanian?" interjected Jess, still sensing he should keep the peace. "Now's the perfect time to talk about Dracula and vampires."

"Don't get me started on Dracula and menstrual blood," said Gilah, pushing away a zealous female fan dressed as Leda being ravished from behind by a large papier-mâché swan. "You know, Nattie, there's something to vampire mythology—your church really goes for it. I don't know about you, but I get really horny when my period's about to start, and that's when I like to bathe my naked body in moonlight, waiting for a vampire."

Jess watched as Gilah placed her hand on the small of Nattie's back, and Nattie flinched but didn't ask her to remove it. He wondered how in hell Gilah found moonlight at The Pierre.

"Yes, I get horny too, and if Jess is lucky, it's a Thursday."

"I think about the two of you on those Thursdays. I'm happy to lend him out every two weeks."

"Just a minute," said Natalia. "Jess and I have been doing this for years. *I'm* lending him out!"

"Please, girls," interjected Jess, flattered. "No need for a competition."

The parade circled around and went down Fifth Avenue, where the thirty-foot skeleton, Ghost of Tom, did his annual danse macabre under Washington Square Arch.

"Could this mean that Tom has gone down at sea?" asked Natalia. Jess sensed she asked this hopefully.

Then they made their way over to Christopher Street, where the tradition was that late-night revelers get naked. They beheld six buff gays take it all off, lock arms, and do a Highland fling. Quickly they moved on.

"Let's go to Tom's townhouse," said Natalia. "It's just a couple of blocks away. There's lots to eat and drink. And there's some weed the previous owner stashed after his religious conversion. Tom and I never use it."

Jess was nervous about which woman he should end up with, so he welcomed Natalia's proposal. He could be neutral. They reached the house on Bethune Street and stumbled up the steps. Natalia switched on the nineteenth-century Baccarat chandelier in the foyer.

Jess had never been inside and felt like an intruder. The brownstone had come ready-made with sumptuous furnishings— American and European period pieces festooned with embroidered accent pillows. The previous owner, a wealthy antiques dealer on East Tenth Street, had had a conversion experience upon reading a book about Zen found by chance at East West Books. He sold everything on the cheap and flew to the Far East in search of spiritual enlightenment. With his uncanny real estate antennae, Tom was the first to bid. Though the ornate beveled mirrors, oriental carpets, Mission and Amish furniture, and Chippendale canopy beds were not to his taste, he made himself at home and went about the business of finding a girlfriend to help him negotiate the twenty-odd rooms.

Natalia found it easy to dodge Tom, given all the rooms, alcoves, and escape hatches. There were even some secret corridors behind bookcases, a dumbwaiter, and a trapdoor under the Persian carpet in the ladies' dressing room. She insisted on a bedroom of her own.

"I'm taking off this padding, back in a second. Off with your masks. Off with that suicide kit, Jess. You won't be needing it tonight!"

It was unusual for Natalia to be so buoyant—the parade seemed to have softened some edges—and Jess's infatuation had shifted over the months more toward Gilah. Now Natalia was revealing aspects of her personality he hadn't fully registered, and he felt Eros swelling toward them both in equal measure. He wondered where this was going.

Love must have food, Lord Byron says, so first they hit the refrigerator and pantry in a kitchen the size of Périgord. "The best parties are always in the kitchen," said Natalia, having changed into a deep-scarlet scoop-neck cashmere sweater and black leggings. "And the best food is always leftovers." She took out a large enameled Cousances cast-iron pot half full of cassoulet, which she reheated on the Franklin stove as the three got into their first bottle of Krug and began the oysters. These Natalia shucked effortlessly.

"Casanova ate twelve dozen at the start of every meal, Jess, before he got to appetizers. It paid off. Try one of these—a Cotuit, from Nantucket." She held the shell to his mouth and he swilled it down.

Gilah pressed her mouth to the pearly shell and the lucky oyster slithered down whole. "That's good, Nattie, let's do more. Lots more!"

They took turns feeding oysters one to another as they stood around the stove. Just as she would with her restaurant peers, Natalia asked for their ratings. Sauce of any kind was against the rules.

"I prefer the Pemaquids to the Pugwashes," said Gilah.

"I prefer the Malpeques to the Chincoteagues," said Jess.

"I prefer the Bluepoints to the Caraquets and all the others," said Natalia. "It's like trying the hundreds of different pastas and then deciding spaghetti is King. Something to say for tradition."

Putting on a French country apron, Natalia stirred the cassoulet and served it up. "Okay, first party game," she said. "It's called name-the-ingredients. Little hint: This is Julia's recipe, modified. She says it's best to spend three days on it but I cut some corners." They sat at the far end of a mahogany dining table for sixteen.

Gilah examined the stew briefly, sniffed the ladle, took a few bites, and put down her fork. "Let's see. Great Northern white beans, pork rind, salt pork, boned pork roast, pork roasting fat, shoulder of New Zealand lamb, cracked lamb bones, Italian parsley, cloves, thyme, garlic—*lots* of garlic—bay leaves, Spanish onions, beef bouillon, dry vermouth, Armagnac—not sure, I think that's Darroze Bas Armagnac Domaine Dupont vintage 1965—white bread crumbs, Dead Sea salt, Tellicherry pepper, chopped white truffles found by pigs the old-fashioned way, braised goose, partridge, a few shotgun pellets, Long Island duck, fresh kill turkey, and, think I'm leaving something out . . . Oh! kielbasa, of course kielbasa! . . . But Nattie, does Polish sausage belong in a Southwestern French stew?"

Silence. Then more silence. Finally, "Jess didn't tell me you knew so much about food, Gilah."

"It's like Polish. I took courses."

"Well, to answer your question, Julia says you can substitute Polish sausage for French in a pinch, so I call this Natalia's Polish

Cassoulet. Tom likes it so much I don't fix much of anything else, even in summer. He ate half this pot just before he left."

The three of them set to devouring the virtuoso stew but after half an hour had hardly made a dent and decided to pass on dessert. They were well into their third bottle of Krug when Natalia produced a joint, lit up, and passed it along to Gilah.

"You're right, Nattie, this is good shit. Can I decide the next party game?"

"You don't need my permission."

"Let's play hide-and-seek—a great way for Jess and me to find all the nooks and crannies."

"I'm game," said Jess. "Who's going to be 'it'?"

"Nattie, you go first. Cover your eyes, and let's play *Bolero* at full volume so you can't hear where we're going. Give us ten minutes."

Natalia took a few moments to refine the rules with respect to keeping score. Then hand in hand, Jess and Gilah scurried up the central winding staircase, quickly checked out the second-floor bedrooms, and ascended via the back stairwell to the servants' quarters on the third floor. In one room, they found Tom's display case of miniature tall ships, a barrel of rum, a log with daily entries of voyages, real and imaginary, and a bunk bed modeled after what you'd find in the captain's quarters of a three-masted ship in the Queen's navy. They lay down on this unforgiving platform and—for what else was there to do?—began making out while they awaited Natalia.

Gilah was even more receptive than usual when Jess kissed the face he built. Was it the oysters? The champagne? The weed? He nibbled at the fake earlobe, left unpierced for fear of polymer destabilization.

"Did a good job on these ears. You still have sensitivity." He ran his fingers over her mane and down to her croup. He fondled her hocks and gaskins and ran his tongue over her poll and caressed her stifle and fetlock and pastern. Then she got on top and asked him to roll over on his belly. "Let me ride you, gimme that dock, gimme! Go Esmeralda!" Jess obliged, not quite remembering what a dock is.

"Gilah, let's get naked. She's not going to find us right away."

"Nothing doing. I'm not easy."

She pressed against him through sequins. "Canter, Es!" He almost threw out his back trying. So far, this night was shaping up dandily. *Bolero* was a trite choice but did its damage. Jess was put in mind of that eighties movie *10*, and hoped he would score maybe a seven, better than his usual five. But which woman, each an improbable ten, would he favor at the end of this party game?

Loud rap at the door. "You're in there, you bad things. I know what you're doing." Natalia strode in and told Gilah to get off her man. She laughed and pulled at Gilah's elbow.

"Well, take him, Nattie. No problem."

Natalia was granted five points under the rules she established and the three reconvened downstairs for the second round of hide-and-seek. This time Gilah was "it."

"Do you mind if we do away with *Bolero*?" asked Natalia. "How about the final act of *Dialogues of the Carmelites*? You know, where all the nuns get their heads chopped off. Great Halloween music."

Her suggestion was taken, and off she went with Jess, while Gilah shut her eyes and smoked another joint.

"Where should we hide?"

Natalia whispered, "Let's do the secret door behind the library shelves—that's where they hid the fugitive slaves. Make lots of noise going up the staircase, then we sneak down the back way. This is fun, just like being kids again."

The library was full of leather-bound books, some of them dating back to the cradle days of printing. The antiquarian dealer bought them as a sideline to his passion for furniture mostly because they enhanced the grandeur of his ceiling-high teak bookcases. Jess found it ironic that this dealer's life was turned around by a five-dollar paperback. It took both of them to pull open the bookcase on its exterior hinges. As in opening a crypt, the slow creaking was just the ticket for Halloween. Pushing aside cobwebs and breathing in the musty air, they pulled the bookcase shut behind them.

"It's pitch-dark. Do you have a flashlight?" Jess asked.

"Just use your imagination. There's little to see. No recent rat sightings in this house, only next door. But you know, it smells like a confessional."

"Go ahead, confess. We've got plenty of time. I'll play priest."

"Well, Father, I confess I like your girlfriend," she whispered as he stood behind her, his arms around her waist. "Do you forgive me?"

"I like her too. But tell me, child, what do you like about her?"

"Not sure. There's something about her voice. Everybody else talks about her looks. So she's a dish, big deal."

"Her voice? Tell me more, child."

"It's deep, sultry. It goes well with her stunning red hair. She speaks with a slight accent I can't quite identify. It's weird—I swear I've heard that voice before . . . It takes me back, makes me feel younger. I confess . . . there's something arousing about it."

As she spoke she pressed her rear against Jess. "There's something arousing about what you're doing, love," he said. "Of course, it's your soul that captivates me. I'm a priest, remember."

"Yes, priests are forbidden to fall in love with body parts."

"Frankly, I worship at the shrine of your . . ." Lingering pudeur prevented his finishing the silly sentence. He reached around to pull her leggings down over the ample flesh, then stopped midway for fear he'd come right then and there, and be a dud for the balance of the evening.

They heard the guillotine doing its work on the nuns. "Forgive me, Father . . . yes Father, I won't tell."

"I hear that! I hear!" cried Gilah on the other side of the bookcase. "I know what you're up to in there." Gilah pulled at the bookshelf and exposed the couple just as Natalia was pulling up her leggings.

Gilah laid claim to the full five points. It was Jess's turn to be "it." He was foggy about the appropriate music, so Gilah decided for him. "Let's play the Indigo Girls—they've just released *Swamp Ophelia*. I brought along a CD, just in case."

"Indigo Girls?"

"You're so out of it, Jess," said Gilah. "Everybody knows them. They're experimental."

"But remember I hate popular music and long walks on the beach."

"Come on, you'll like this. Now give us at least twenty minutes." She took Natalia by the elbow.

As Gilah and Natalia hurried off, Jess listened to the Indigo Girls singing something about getting more than they'd bargained for.

He thought, *In a way, yes.* He'd been slipping through life after the tough years of being a foster child without anchorage, ignorant of his biological parents and baffled by the enigma of who he was. Now he had two girlfriends, neither insisting on marriage, and that made things easy, sort of. They even liked each other. As for marriage, all the couples he'd lived with returned him to the agency, and they all had iffy ways of dealing with mutual contempt, like group sex and taking in foster kids as distractions or income boosts. Why imitate them in holy matrimony? And though he didn't like to think he had much in common with other bachelors, he valued a certain open-endedness, like the vistas that Santa Fe offered in his youth. Marriage seemed like permanently locking in a Jess Freeman he was dissatisfied with. But, unlike Natalia with her sentiments about wedlock, he didn't totally rule it out.

Dissatisfied with himself? Yes, something was missing whenever he said his own name, some hole in the fabric that *plastic surgeon* didn't fill. Gilah had dragged him to a lecture by an English prof at the New School who spoke of John Keats and how identity comes about through buffeting with circumstance—we suck our identity from the human heart as it suffers loss, pain, blocked desire. Smart boy, that Keats. Maybe Jess was shielding his own heart from the torments of love and jealousy. Maybe he should break through his trance-laden escapism, commit to one of these women.

He thought about Alison and the handful of other women he'd pursued over the years. Maybe he was chasing armadillos, only imagining he was in love with real-life humans. Maybe he sent subtle hints to them that he didn't want their passion, their devotion, for he was in a world elsewhere of his own making where he preferred to stay. Was this why they were always backing away, and he was left alone, not joining in life's feast?

In his trances there was a priestess with mesmeric green eyes, whose vanishings made him hunger. She too was distant, always receding down dark passageways, but beckoning. He tried to retain her by fabricating objects such as small tapestries of Southeastern desert landscapes or miniature oases or portraits of her in green and gold painted on old plywood. Sometimes these reminded him of the face he shaped for Margaret Epstein. Other times they resembled a sphinx who terrified him, from whose eyes a coil would emerge to pierce and kill him. *I have to pinch myself out of this trance*, he would think, as he returned in full consciousness to an eyelid procedure or chin tuck.

He knew his trances were a deflection from reality, but sometimes they were a metamorphosis of reality into radiant wish fulfillment. Whichever, they were a compensation for something missing in his own sense of identity, he now figured, beginning with his parentage. For what was he? Jess Freeman was a fragment, an enigma, and his William Blake syndrome was likely a symptom of it, telling him he needed somehow to become whole. Maybe wholeness was within reach with one of these remarkable women. It was time to break out of his mind-forged manacles.

All this serious rumination left a small hitch: *Which woman?*

Just then The Indigo Girls were singing "Dead Man's Hill." Didn't bode well. Time to look for the women. He stood up, a little dizzy, and set out. He decided against the obvious places—the alcoves, closets, bedrooms. Natalia would know where the really good hiding places were. Let's see, there was that trapdoor under the rug in the ladies' dressing room. Since furniture was atop the rug, it took some effort to move things, roll the rug up, and open the trapdoor. Nobody there. Then it struck him—that was really dim! How could they have replaced the furniture if they were hiding under the floor? *I must be losing it*, he thought. *Better not go into a trance.*

The Indigo Girls sang "Fare thee well" while he looked into the dumbwaiter, checked out the billiard room, and stuck his nose into the larder. He had just found an opening to the attic when he heard an angry shriek from the master bedroom at the rear of the second floor. Terrified, he ran to it, opened the door, and beheld a scene well in progress.

In a large canopied bed, Natalia was naked and backed up against a bedpost while Gilah was facing her on all fours, her long red hair draped on the sheets.

Natalia screamed, "Nipple ring! Spider tattoo! Yes, your voice, I'd know it anywhere. I know who you are, *Irma Frumkin*! *How dare you?*"

"You mean Margaret Epstein?" asked Jess.

"Margaret Epstein, who's that? This is Irma Frumkin. Gilah de Champigny, sure, and I'm Joan of Arc . . . Jess, are you in on this?"

"Well, kind of . . . like sort of. But Gilah really likes you, so what's the problem?"

"I'll tell you the problem. Irma Frumkin is a stalker. I met her at Bronx Community College the year before I met you. Was sent there to convince young losers that there were opportunities in life. She came up afterward and I couldn't shake her. Bitch!"

"But Gilah, you went to Jacobson Sinai Academy in Miami and Smith College," said Jess, standing limply at the door.

Gilah whimpered a little and rolled over on her side. She pulled up a sheet to cover her naked back and behind.

"Sinai Academy, Smith College, are you kidding?" said Natalia. "Her father was a plumber, her mother a seamstress. She's from the Bronx."

"But what about all those equestrian trophies? She learned to ride at the finest academies, and those places aren't cheap."

"She hung out at cop stables and drove those pitiful buggies for tourists in Central Park. That's where she learned about horses.

Okay, she learned well, I'm sure the trophies are for real. But did you ever think to look at the inscriptions? I'll bet they say *Irma Frumkin*."

"She doesn't let me into her suite—"

"Jess told me you live at The Pierre. How long have you lived there?" This with deep sarcasm. "Last I heard, you were doing a share with three slut stewardesses in a tenement on the Lower East Side."

"Go easy, Nattie. I don't see what all the fuss is about." Jess approached them gingerly and sat down on the bedside. "It occurs to me you must have been friendly with Gilah early on or you wouldn't know about her nipple ring."

Silence from Natalia.

Gilah began to speak, slowly, softly at first, then more emphatically. "Okay, I'm from the South Bronx. I'm . . . Irma Frumkin. My parents were poor working-class Jews. Until five months ago I didn't live at The Pierre. I'd circle back on the subway to the Markle women's home on Thirteenth Street after Jess left me. I was living in a place that keeps hymens intact—curfews and no men allowed. You had nuns, Nattie, I had the Salvation Army. Got the nipple ring and tattoo as my little mutinies. Thanks to your Tom, I launched the Champigny line, and now I really do live in The Pierre, Suite 2121. I changed my name to Margaret Epstein after the fiasco with you. Figured I needed a new start. It didn't work. I couldn't forget you."

"What fiasco?" asked Jess.

"I'll tell this in my own way," said Gilah. "Take your hands off my butt."

"Sorry."

Gilah went into a lotus position and lit up a joint.

"I escaped the Bronx public schools with just some minor cigarette burns and didn't go to City College. I was programmed for Bronx Community. Majored in accounting and was resigned to working at Kmart. But I was a dreamer and most of my dreams were horses. I'd hang out at cop stables—Nattie got that part right. And yes, I had my first orgasm on a horse, but she wasn't an Arabian named Esmeralda, she was a mangy nag named Beulah. We liked each other, and she did her last canter just for me. That's when Natalia Wojciechowski entered the picture."

"Well, you still say my name nicely."

"You were billed as a young journalist who carved out a career against the odds, so I showed up at your lecture and sat in the first row. You had great looks and a fabulous body, though you wore really dumb shoes. You had everything we wanted—and your freedom. You weren't married, and we liked that because we'd have to accept the first icky proposal to come along—there might not be another. Especially for me. I was no looker. Sought out some lesbian action in the West Village but never lucked out. You were relaxed and funny but inspirational—if you could do it, we could do it. I felt tingles while you talked about your career and all the things you wanted to do. You weren't always going to be a restaurant reviewer. You were out to drain the dregs of life. But you also said you believed in rules, life wasn't chaos, we had to follow our conscience and not let others jerk us around."

"Have to say, I didn't think the talk was going all that well."

"Well it did. Next day I switched from accounting to journalism. You remember after your talk I told you I'd do anything to be your apprentice. I could spell well enough and needed to get out of the Bronx. I think you just wanted to get me off your back. But you gave me your card. I still have it. I slept with it that night, kissed it because your hand touched it, pressed it against my breasts."

"You know, Irma—I mean Gilah—in journalism we're taught that when we launch a word we can't take it back," said Natalia. "It makes its own way, it may cause damage. Guess I shouldn't have given you my card... Sorry about that." She moved her hand tentatively toward Gilah's left knee.

Gilah continued. "So yes, I was a mess. Pretty much ignored by both sexes. But I know this much—*we are lived by our passions.* I couldn't control what happened the next few months. I was in love with you, Nattie... And I still am!" She sobbed, broke out of her lotus, and threw herself on Natalia's lap.

Natalia put her hands on Gilah's beautiful head, massaged it, and breathed deeply. Jess feared an evening that had begun well was going to hell. To fill the silence he asked, "Uh, was that you I saw in Café Loup and McSorley's?"

Gilah caught her breath. "Yes, and that was me on the Ferris wheel. I wore wigs and other disguises so Nattie wouldn't spot me. I learned disguise from her, you see. Nice irony. And in case she ever softened toward me, I learned Polish, I practiced eating Polish grub, I took courses at the Culinary Institute, I studied Central European history and culture. I joined Claremont and rode Polish horses. I was better at riding than stalking, and some of my trophies say Margaret Epstein, not Irma Frumkin. Yes, I stalked her after we had sex—for five years. When she reported me to the police, I just took greater precautions. I've been stalking the two of you on your fuck Thursdays for years. I hang out at the Waverly Inn across the street. I watch when Nattie arrives, and when she leaves I see how she looks. It makes me jealous as hell."

"Did you just say something about sex?" asked Jess.

"I'll get to that—sit tight. Nattie, you talk about my Bronx upbringing like you've always lived in a château. But remember, you grew up on Tompkins Square and ate blood soup and tripe. You're like me. But at least my pop didn't poison himself with pierogi—he lived well enough until he drowned in a sewer. Look Nattie, we started poor and now we're rich bitches. Let's unite for class revenge! What do you see in Tom anyway? You don't need a sugar daddy. I won't ask what you see in Jess here." She pinched him, hard.

"Ouch!"

Natalia sighed. "Okay, I'm back in the confessional. Should be obvious it's *because* Tom is so ineligible . . . Still, I like him, he's got brash charm. And he has this townhouse. I may be well off but I'm no tycoon—who in hell doesn't need a townhouse?" Her face twitched. She knew this was a feeble defense. "I've got a question for you, Gilah. How did you get to be so damned beautiful?"

Gilah told the story of her fall from the horse—yes, a Polish horse. No, she hadn't planned to make a mess of her face but in the ambulance she quickly concocted a plot for turning calamity to some advantage. She knew Jess had famously stitched up the mayor and, after years of stalking Natalia, she knew he was her best chance of getting into her inner circle.

"I'm surprised you turned out so well," said Jess. "I haven't been able to pull this off with any of my other clients. Maybe someday you'll tell the world your story so I can use you in my promos?"

"I'm the one who used you. Sorry, Jess—I had sex with you because you were having sex with Nattie. When I was with you, it was only two degrees of separation. That was the turn-on. You were my way of getting to Nattie, taking her back . . ."

Jess knew he should be outraged to hear that he had been used in this way, but on some level it flattered him. He had been a conduit of passion, if not the object of it. This was a larger role in the romantic life than he usually played. And he felt a certain empathy with Irma-Margaret-Gilah, for she had practiced love at a distance, his problem too.

"Look at my nipple ring," Gilah said. She bared her left breast. Natalia took a candle and peered along with Jess, who had never looked at it closely. Delicately engraved on the outer rim was *Natalia*. "I had it inscribed shortly after we made love. And it wasn't just once, you know. We met at Ophelia's every night for a week. Then you just stopped showing up." She breathed deeply.

Without saying anything, Natalia touched Gilah's breast and gently kissed it.

"God, Nattie," moaned Gilah. Nattie turned her head and rested it against Gilah's breast. "Do you remember when we made love that first night?" Gilah asked. "I'd only to been to Ophelia's once before." She looked at Jess. "It's got three floors, like Dante. Yes, I read him because he's even more Catholic than Nattie. Except hell was at the top and anything goes in hell, you know. The first floor was a piano bar—that was heaven. The second was dirty dancing—purgatory. The third was—well, you remember, Nattie. You tell him."

Natalia sighed again. "You asked me to meet you at the right spot—you knew I'd go for the heaven-hell stuff. It was like being a bad Catholic girl, badder than ever. We did all three floors, drinking vodka martinis and listening to that transvestite singing Sinatra, then upstairs for dirty dancing to the soundtrack of *Dirty Dancing*. We danced—you were better than I. I'm all feet and clunked around but you didn't care. Then you wanted to explore the third floor. There were mirrors everywhere, including the ceiling, and there was incense and the floor was padded and, hate to say it, they were playing *Bolero*. There were little booths and we parted some curtains and saw two women in striped socks doing it."

While Natalia was speaking, Gilah had moved up to her side and was stroking her inner thigh through the sheet. Natalia continued, "You wanted to go into a booth of our own. I was eager all of a sudden—I'd always heard stories at St. Brigid's that nuns do it too—and I was drunk."

Jess watched Gilah stroking her, Natalia slowly moving her hips. "Then . . . please say it, Nattie. What happened next."

"You were on top—I liked your long face, I really did, and your black eyes got to me. You kissed me. I couldn't believe it was happening. You said you were in love with me . . . and I said I was in love with you." Natalia stopped to catch her breath. But Gilah's hand was now under the sheet.

"Then you unbuttoned my blouse," Gilah said. "And messed for a time with my bra—I reached around and undid it. You kissed my breasts. Surprised you with my nipple ring. You unzipped my skirt and touched my tattoo and pulled down your Levis and pressed against me. And after just a few minutes, we started coming, and we came and came!" Gilah was now under the sheet with Natalia.

Jess just sat there, watching Gilah's flexed muscles as she pressed down, and seeing the rapture on Natalia's face just before she cried out, "Oh, Irma, I still love you, love you, I'll always love you!"

— Part Two —

THE SUMMER OF '61

— Chapter Eight —

CHANGES

Tom Langley perished at sea that Halloween in 1995 trying to outwit a squall. He had willed the townhouse on Bethune Street to Natalia. After she mourned a decent three months—she truly missed him in her own way for he was likable and had been generous—she invited Gilah to move in. Both women stopped having sex with Jess, though they wished to keep him as their close friend and of course he should frequently join them for dinner. Seven years passed.

During this time Jess went through a spell of wishing to use Dr. Kevorkian's kit. Just as he'd been connecting with these two women in what felt like reciprocal love for the first time, they'd pushed him aside. In keeping with the spirit of the times, he acknowledged it might be payback for centuries of male oppression and myopia.

Myopia, yes, but he didn't think himself macho. In a personality test Harvard forced him to take, he'd scored in the eighty-fourth percentile in femininity, eclipsing many Radcliffe women. Weren't other men—guys who valued ice hockey, Bud Light, and all-you-can-eat buffets—more suitable targets for gender payback?

He didn't exactly declare for celibacy but found that in his midthirties, when testosterone still raged, he was shunning sex with others and retreating into a masturbatory bubble where sex with phantoms of his alternative universe relieved temporarily the cruel seminal pressure. In most other respects, he'd had it with sex. Would the curse of Alison ever be lifted?

These seven years were not without incident. One day Jess was served a summons by Stem, Fitzgerald, and Stern naming him defendant in a malpractice suit. The plaintiff was the former mayor, who claimed his defeat in the last election was owing to a collapse of the plastic surgery Jess performed. Jess had noticed that previously revised scar tissue was presenting vividly, especially on high-definition television, and that some features seemed adrift on the mayor's face. He never paraded his gifts as a plastic surgeon, but at the time of his initial work on the despot he was much applauded, and his practice flourished. The mayor asked two million in physical damages and an equal sum for the mental pain and suffering of being put out to pasture. A team of paid plastic surgeons and psychiatrists was on tap to back up the mayor's claims, widely publicized in tabloids.

HIZZONER $AVES FACE!
NIP AND SCHMUCK: VILLAGE DOC SUED FOR
PRETTY PENNY!!

Fortunately, Natalia's friend Horace Holliday was a lawyer who specialized in defending doctors in malpractice suits. They plotted their strategy over raw eel with Natalia's gang at Nobu.

"It's a little worrisome," said Jess. "Remember he beat those assault and battery charges after the pub brawl."

"Yes," said Horace, "and all the bribery and corruption charges too. But I'm confident we'll win on liability. You didn't solicit those surgeries. Nobody else could be found at the time."

"And have I told you how hard it is to work up to standard when the patient has been eating steak-and-kidney pie?"

These arguments prevailed in New York City Civil Court where Horace presented the case to the six jurors, fully deploying his rhetorical chops in describing the ordeal from the perspective of a put-upon surgeon. He ridiculed the analogy used by the plaintiff's lawyers that what had purported to be, in the mayor's reconstructed face, a lavish early twentieth-century Southampton seaside manor was actually a shabby post–World War II prefab, destined to fall apart at the seams.

"Some of us cannot afford manors and must settle for prefabs. Why should the mayor be any different?"

Horace declined his usual fee. This was pro bono work for a friend.

Horace had undergone a transformation of his own over the years. He never disguised his sexual orientation but would complain that he was no good at being gay. For one thing, there was the challenge of his obesity. Gays didn't demand that he be buff, but a waistline of eighty-six was a lot to get around. So his sex life was largely vicarious. He was in love, he claimed, with a young Russian émigré named Sergei, who led a mostly straight life and kept Horace informed of his conquests of rich Upper East Side widows.

"Sergei sounds like a prick-tease to me," said Natalia to Horace over dinner one evening at Prune, where the signature fruit appeared in virtually every dish, like it or not. "And why would tales of het-sex be a turn-on for you, anyway?"

"My therapist encourages me to listen—he says I might turn this gay thing around someday. It's called conversion therapy."

Nobody at the table was so blunt as to suggest that obesity might be disqualifying in the eyes of some women as well. Jess thought that maybe Horace guessed this, because to give himself a fighting chance whichever way he might swing, he got his stomach stapled. The surgery worked. Though he continued the weekly judgmental feasts, he took only tiny bites after a day of tiny bites. A dramatic shrinkage began, and he went from waist 86 to 62 to 42 to 34 in one year. Jess sent him to a colleague who specialized in flaying giant folds of excess skin. He could have tried the surgery himself, but both he and Horace worried that maybe the mayor's lawyers were right.

Then Horace joined Crunch Fitness on East Thirteenth Street. Every day, early morning and late afternoon, he showed up for the StairMaster, the weight machines, the pool, and a quarter hour of abdominals supervised by a trainer named Ray, who asked intrusive cool-down questions of everyone in the class. "Now tell us something about yourself that nobody wants to know." "When did you start lying to your parents?" "How will you cheat on your diet today?"

Schooled as a lawyer, Horace never told the truth anyway. He began creating a version of himself for the class, a strategy that put Jess in mind of Gilah. In this he was encouraged by his therapist, who believed that instead of bringing repressed truths to the surface, his clients should plaster reality over with more palatable versions of themselves. He called this *therapeutic self-refashioning.* Given enough sessions on the couch, his clients would come to believe their own elaborate fibs.

Horace's responses to Ray's questions bore small resemblance to fact, as he confessed to Jess. Instead of gay, he was a ladies' man, keeping a fluid list of girlfriends since elementary school. No, he was never fat, he just needed some stretching and toning. Yes, he was a lawyer, but he specialized in pro bono work for the disabled. No, he took little interest in transvestite burlesque.

He and Jess started going off for another round of drinks after they accompanied Gilah and Natalia back to the townhouse on Bethune. Horace would order lime spritzers and Jess that Mexican liqueur with a dead worm at the bottom, a carryover from his Santa Fe days. Horace inducted Jess into various forms of higher culture— the Metropolitan Opera, the Chelsea art scene, and especially the ballet. It was no longer the heyday of the seventies, when people died for Balanchine, Suzanne Farrell, and Baryshnikov, and when a dance belt of Nureyev was rumored to be circulating in the gay underground. But Horace found vestiges of greatness in the New York City Ballet and took the philosophical position that it was the same company, even though its dancers, musicians, designers, and artistic director had all changed.

Jess regarded these activities with Horace as *man dates*—defined by the *New York Times* as male bonding over dinner and through cultural events, with no talk of sports or sex. Males on man dates were not to share a bottle of wine, but rather to order their own wine of choice by the glass. This maintained proper male distance. But Jess noted with some unease that whenever they dined out, Horace would insist on breaking that cardinal rule—and the two would share an expensive bottle of burgundy. Jess would consume most of it out of respect for Horace's new waistline. Thus their friendship developed.

Jess had had a few male friends. There was fifth-grader Jim Hensley, who ate hotdogs sideways and pinned Jess to the ground with the same slobbery French kisses he gave his Basset hound. Then eighth-grader Ricky Stumpf, who taught him how to steal chewing gum and skinny-dip in the flash floods that frequented New Mexico. And there was high school senior Walt Franklin. They visited Albuquerque on a lark. Walt called Jess "man" all the time and, wearing a white sheet, sneaked up on him at a urinal in the local YMCA, so terrifying him that Jess never again used urinals. And there was his Harvard classmate, Gilbert Hilbert, who was married to a spirited Latvian feminist and sought out Jess's company. Gilbert had been studying philosophy, so they discussed profound matters at the Oxford Grill in Harvard Square, such as whether God gave a damn or whether Virginia Woolf had the right idea when she weighted her bloomers and stepped into the sea. In his last communication with Jess, Gilbert wrote that he had left his spouse and accepted a tutorship in philosophy at Oxford, where he intended to pursue "a life of serious buggery."

Jess eventually saw a pattern here of his submissiveness to the Male Will. He was not proud of his dealings with male friends. So he was on guard during these man dates with Horace. Not that he was homophobic, but he thought it better not to give false encouragement.

Horace would talk about his still frustrated love for Sergei, who gave up conning Upper East Side widows for identity theft. Horace made partner in his firm and took frequent vacations on the Italian Riviera. He sent Jess photographs of himself richly tanned and buff and wearing a Speedo, always with a note saying that his extreme makeover was paying off in ways he could never have imagined— and with both sexes. He'd love to tell Jess all about it, just as Sergei had told him all. But whenever Horace returned, Jess was careful not to ask. Instead they would discuss, yes, whether God gave a damn and whether Virginia Woolf had the right idea when she weighted her bloomers and stepped into the sea.

During this period Natalia and Gilah prospered professionally. Though she still wrote her astringent food column and published two controversial anti-fusion cookbooks with Knopf, Natalia became editor of the city section of the *New York Times* Sunday edition and a major cultural arbiter on such issues as whether the Jefferson Market Library should sacrifice elderly reading space to rowdy teenagers, or whether Kush, a hookah bar on Chrystie Street, should retain its patina of tobacco juice on the walls of the men's room.

For her part, Gilah saw her fame become international, eclipsing Natalia's and rivaling that of the Olsen twins and Kate Moss. Her line of beauty products gave Estée Lauder heartburn and they were politically correct to boot, with no animal testing and five percent of revenues donated to a charity for endangered wild horses. But it was as a supermodel in her early thirties that she entered the ranks of the top celebs. She fought the stereotype that supermodels were airheads who, like Beverly Johnson, believed that "everyone should have enough money to get plastic surgery." Unlike Linda Evangelista, she was willing to get out of bed every morning for less than ten grand. And she declined to sell her eggs to rich infertile couples. She rapidly became the Jean-Paul Sartre of supermodels. "Existence precedes essence," she said casually in an interview, and the slogan appeared on the cover of *Elle* as if it were her own. Figuring out what she meant led to a revival of philosophical discourse in fashion magazines.

One Thursday afternoon in early December 2002, Jess received a call from Natalia asking him to meet her at the Cedar Tavern on University Place. Because it was a Thursday, his heart leapt. Could she be pondering a renewal of their late-afternoon rendezvous? She was awaiting him in a booth near the kitchen, wearing a scarlet cashmere sweater and black leggings, much like what she had changed into that Halloween eve seven years earlier. He envied the bench she sat on.

"You know the history of this tavern, don't you, Jess? It was the hangout for the New York School—you know, Motherwell, Pollock, Guston, de Kooning, Kline. Also the Beats—Ginsberg, Kerouac, Corso. Lee Krasner hated it because it was a guy place, and Frank O'Hara hated it because Pollock called him a fag here."

For once, Jess already knew some of this, or thought he did. "Yes—look, we're sitting next to Pollock's graffiti," he said, pointing to the painter's name carved into the wood with bold letters. "It's like Lord Byron carving his name in the Greek temple at Sounion. I guess some desecrations enhance the value of the pop stand."

"Hate to tell you, it's not the same tavern. The old Cedar Tavern was down the street at 24 University Place, and at two other places before that. We're at 82. That graffiti is fake. This place is pretending to be itself. Still, it *is* history—sort of."

"Okay, so we're back to the identity enigma," said Jess. "Is this or is this not the same tavern?"

They ordered hamburgers medium rare with bacon. He heard her sigh.

"So Nattie, why'd you want to see me?"

"It's Gilah. You know her better than anybody else, so I thought I'd run this by you . . . I'm afraid she's got the seven-year itch."

"That's surprising. Uh, any evidence?"

"No smoking gun yet, thank God. But some things have been changing in our routine."

"Like what?"

"You'll laugh. Mostly it's just a feeling I have. You know, the kind of thing men are really dumb at."

"Some of us have the occasional insight."

"She used to bring me extravagant black orchids and purple thistles from Very Special Flowers on West Tenth. Now she gets wilted snapdragons from the Korean deli around the corner."

"Well, don't overinterpret—"

"When she used to go on photo shoots to Costa Rica or Madagascar, she'd call me every three hours. Now I'm lucky to hear from her once a day." She thumped her fingers on the table.

"Well, that does hurt, I guess."

"She used to show up by eight o'clock for one of our rare stay-at-home dinners. In the early days I pulled out all the stops. Not cassoulet. I worked hard to serve what a supermodel could eat—like sautéed scallops with broccoletti di rapa or Roman vegetable casserole with artichokes and fava beans or roast squab on liver canapés. We'd dress up and light candles with a real sense of occasion for no reason at all except we were in love. Then we'd have great sex until two in the morning, no matter what appointment we had a few hours later with *The Morning Show* or Knopf. But now she shows up late with no excuse, her mascara's a mess, she seems distracted. Actually a bigger appetite than usual, but she forgets to compliment my cooking. And she's switched her scent from the Jicky I gave her to L'Heure Bleue. And then there's our sex life . . ."

"Yes, your, uh . . ." Jess felt a twinge.

"We used to do it all the time—nine or ten times a week even when we were tired. It's not like living with Tom all over again, but we're lucky to do it twice a week now. And something else has changed."

"Oh?"

"You know about girl-on-girl action, right? I was femme, she was butch. I was the bottom, she was the top. Now she wants it the other way around. I liked it better when she did me. Now it's up to me to do things that arouse her—and I've exhausted the inventory at Babeland. What do you think, Jess? Is this the Gilah you knew? She dumped you, I guess she could dump me."

Jess wasn't sure, but it didn't sound good. "Do you think fame has gone to her head? Celebs all have groupies, sometimes they're hard to resist. Or so I've heard." This wasn't what Natalia wanted to hear. He caught her frown and continued, "Look, Nattie, no one could hold a candle to you. If she *is* roaming, she'll come back. But we don't even know—maybe it's one of those change-of-life things."

"At thirty-three, doctor?"

"Come to think of it, she's got another couple of decades. Okay, maybe we should just monitor this awhile, not jump to conclusions."

"I've thought of snooping or even stalking but I'm afraid of what I might find."

"Stalking? That's role reversal!"

"I'm entitled."

They dug into their burgers. "You know there's been some talk about you and Horace," Natalia said. "One member of our group—won't say who—thinks the two of you are a couple. Want to tell me, for old times' sake?"

"There's something else I'd rather do for old times' sake, Nattie, but you're not in the mood. See how intuitive I am? No, Horace and I are just friends—I've made that clear to him. But there's one thing I confess. We share a bottle of burgundy on our man dates."

"Uh-oh, that's breaking the rules."

Jess and Natalia didn't see each other again for a couple of weeks, until the epicures reconvened, this time at Sammy's Roumanian on Chrystie Street. A basement restaurant with garish fluorescent lights, Sammy's was *the* place in town for Jewish food and vaudevillian disco. The walls were plastered over with yellowed photographs and pennants and old clippings from Yiddish newspapers. Every night was like a Jewish wedding, with a tummler who told Jewish jokes and sang Hebrew and Yiddish songs while playing an electronic keyboard. There was always lots of audience participation, including dancing the hora, no matter how saturated with chicken fat everybody was. And patrons didn't place orders, they just sat back and waited for the chopped chicken liver, pickles, kreplach, latkes, and stuffed cabbage, then sweetbreads, sliced brains, skirt steak, and meatballs, all this smothered with schmaltz, poured terrifyingly by waiters holding pitchers three feet above the plates. To cut the fat, liters of vodka were served in blocks of ice, and no table escaped with fewer than two bottles. This was topped off by chocolate egg creams, which waiters showed patrons how to make for themselves with siphon bottles of seltzer.

Too bad that parties of eight were then served with a $1,200 tab, not including gratuities for the waiters and tummler. Wasn't all this just for fun? But Natalie's gang didn't have to worry—*Times* subscribers were paying for everything, whether the food was fit to eat or not.

A pair of diners at the mike was doing an old Mel Brooks–Carl Reiner routine.

"Sir, you're two thousand forty-two years old—how, may I ask, have you managed to look so good?"

"Brussels sprouts."

"Brussels sprouts?"

"That's right. I never ate them."

Jess blinked as he took it all in, but Gilah was in her element. "Restaurant of my people," she said.

Jess noted that Gilah, arriving late, had the option of sitting next to Natalia, who was in her Groucho Marx disguise, but instead sat next to Sumalee, a winsome Thai in her late thirties who specialized in Eastern cuisine and wore delicate silks passed down from her great-grandmother. Sure enough, Gilah seemed to be flirting with her. Sumalee was having trouble with the food as well as the din but clearly wished to be as multicultural as possible.

"Come on, Sumie, just try it," said Gilah, tilting a fork laden with Romanian broilings toward the Thai beauty. "It's karnatzlach, you know, garlic sausage. Jews know what you really like. Just open, Sumie, come on now, try it!" Sumie gamely gulped it down, quickly putting a napkin to her lips.

Natalia and Jess sat together on the other side of the table.

"Maybe she's just being friendly," said Jess.

"But why does she look at Sumalee's lips instead of her eyes?"

"It's loud in here. She's reading them."

After a string of Yiddish one-liners, the tummler announced it was time for the hora. Up sprang Gilah and reached for Sumalee.

"Dude, I don't *do* the hora!" she protested.

"It's easy. I'll teach you!"

The reluctant Thai joined the circle, holding hands with Gilah and a prosthodontist from the Bronx. Sumalee caught on to the step quickly and was soon the equal of her instructor in twists, turns, and communal feeling. Natalia and Jess joined in, but Jess could see that his partner was out of humor.

When they sat down, the tummler announced they had a celebrity in the room. "No, I don't mean Groucho Marx over there. Gilah de Champigny, would you please step forward and favor the company with some wisecracks?"

Gilah took the mike and announced that instead of wisecracks she would sing a couple of songs learned as a teenager in Hebrew camp at Zionsville, Indiana. "I'd like to dedicate the first one to an aspiring Jew at my table, Sumalee Kanokratlananukul." Laughter.

Taking the mike from the stand she approached Sumalee and sang:

I have compared thee, O my love,
to a company of horses in Pharaoh's chariots.
Thy cheeks are comely with rows of jewels,
thy neck with chains of gold.
Thy navel is like a round goblet,
which wanteth not liquor.
Thy belly is like an heap of wheat
set about with lilies.
Thy two breasts are like two young roes
that are twins,
which feed among the lilies.

Sumalee led the warm applause.

"And now," said the tummler, "how about a song for the famed food critic Natalia Wojciechowski? Sorry to blow your cover, Miss Wojciechowski, but they already served the food and it's too late to make it any better." Laughter. Gilah approached Natalia and sang:

Set me as a seal upon thine heart,
as a seal upon thine arm:
for love is as strong as death;
Jealousy is cruel as the grave:
The coals thereof are coals of fire,
which hath a most vehement flame.

Natalia squirmed and frowned. There was no applause. Jess took the opportunity to look at Gilah's face in the bright fluorescent light. He looked again. Then he took his napkin to his eyeglasses and looked yet again.

Something was wrong.

One of her celebrated cheekbones—the right malar plane—seemed to have slipped downward maybe five millimeters. And the right eye appeared now to be not quite on the same latitude with the left. And the forcible Joan Crawford chin appeared to have receded the width of perhaps seven human hairs.

Nobody else in the room could have registered the changes, but Jess blinked, shuddered, and reached for the seltzer.

— Chapter Nine —

PHANTOM LOVERS

Amanda Morley had a contract with Avon to write a how-to book based on the life of Edna St. Vincent Millay, poet and Greenwich Village denizen in the Bohemian era of the twenties and thirties. Edna's poetry, in and out of favor over the years, was overshadowed by her remarkable life, and Amanda's job, as Jess would later learn, was to bring that life up to date and tell us how Edna's life could change ours. If this could be done with so unwieldy an instrument as Proust, why not Millay, whose unorthodox behavior was upfront in all its badness? She drank, smoked, and did drugs, was bisexual and preferred being called *Vincent* over *Edna*. She let herself be photographed having sex next to a swimming pool, coveted an ivory dildo, had abortions, was a pacifist, wrote poems—and worse, she read them in public. She was impassioned about everything, burning her candle, she said famously, at both ends. Amanda's working title was *The New Bohemianism: How Edna St. Vincent Millay Can Tell You What You Need to Know About Sex, Love, and Choices*.

With her $20,000 advance, twenty-eight-year-old Amanda moved into the three-story red brick townhouse at 75 1/2 Bedford Street, where Millay herself had lived and written from 1923 to 1924. It was January of 2004. In many ways Amanda had little in common with Millay. She was the daughter of an alcoholic naval contractor in

San Diego, whose wife left him to live in sin with a Presbyterian minister down the block. Amanda grew up with her mother's encouragement to keep a journal—and this she did from adolescence onward, modeling it on the diaries of Anaïs Nin without the kind of saucy material Anaïs had at her fingertips in Greenwich Village. So it became a largely fictitious journal with lovers of both sexes and journeys to all seven continents. She majored in English at UCLA, took creative writing at Stanford, and intended to write novels but switched to the field dubbed *creative nonfiction*. Writing about Edna St. Vincent Millay was a way of continuing her engagement with deeply expressive women who happened to live in Greenwich Village, while at the same time not working on Anaïs Nin, whose guts she had come to hate.

Amanda occupied the garret where Millay had holed up and set to work. The townhouse had the distinction of being the skinniest in Manhattan—only nine and a half feet wide—and was within easy reach of Chumley's at 86 Bedford, one of the few surviving speakeasies, if doomed to collapse in 2007. Around the corner on Commerce Street was the Cherry Lane Theatre, a box factory until Millay and others converted it into a theater in 1923, graced by the likes of Edward Albee, Sam Shepard, Harold Pinter, and Lanford Wilson. Across the way were stately townhouses with mansard roofs and, at Bedford and Grove streets, the oldest Dutch houses in town. Nearby on Hudson Street stood the 1820 Episcopal Church of St. Luke in the Field, where for decades imperious cats held sway over an untidy garden, even as the rectors failed to hold sway over their congregation. This was the heart of the heart of the West Village, and Amanda was here to pluck the heart out of Millay and serve it up on a how-to platter.

Unlike previous biographers and critics of Millay, Amanda updated research methods and, following the practice of all twenty-first-century undergraduates, did most of her work on the internet. That she herself was writing a *book*—a throwback to print culture—was a little irony she enjoyed.

And this, by chance, was how she came to know Jess. Part of her research meant finding out how to deal with depression. Millay had her own methods, such as sleeping around and winning the Pulitzer Prize at an early age. What was there to learn here? Amanda decided to enter chat rooms where depressives might be found, and registered at worldwearie.com. Here, one evening, she texted back and forth with someone who called himself Befuddled. She herself adopted the nom de plume Meddlesome.

Meddlesome: *Sure you didn't bring this on yourself? Sounds like the signs were there from the beginning. Natasha was cold. Mildred sounded like a lesbian. Couldn't see this coming? Maybe it's what you really wanted.*

Jess was trying to protect intimates by not texting real names. He had thrown his lot in with worldwearie.com at the suggestion of a Botox patient who said he looked even more depressed than she.

Befuddled: *But I've never known what I really want. That's the problem. I think I'm straight, I want to be in an enduring relationship, I'm presentable, I've got credentials and a floor-through on Bank Street, so what's my problem?*

Meddlesome: *You think you're straight?*

Befuddled: *There's this one guy—let's call him André. A lawyer, my closest guy friend, and I'm afraid he's been courting me for many years. Natasha and Mildred are calling me a prick-tease. That's also what they call André's boyfriend—Valdar—he's into identity theft— exciting to a lawyer, I guess. But he never puts out.*

Meddlesome: *Poor André. Sounds like he's not getting any. Maybe you should find a new girlfriend or two.*

Befuddled: *Maybe, but how? I'm forty-two.*

Meddlesome: *That's old but not all that old. I meet somebody new every two weeks, mostly men, at nerve.com. Some of them are even older than you. But it's not for relationships—usually two nights. Sex with a stranger, then a farewell fuck.*

Befuddled: *Sounds scary. What do you get out of it?*

Meddlesome: *You find out the most intimate thing about a person in three hours, then you call it off after one more fuck for old times' sake. But it's also research. I'm writing about a slutty poet, and I need to know what it felt like. This is the age of the hookup.*

Jess had pudeur enough to be shocked by all this, but Meddlesome intrigued him, and over the next few weeks they frequently met in the chat room but went off to a room of their own that worldwearie.com facilitated. One night, in an alcoholic stupor, he texted his true name and profession and, worse, the names of Natalia, Gilah, Horace, and Sergei.

Natalia Wojciechowski, Gilah de Champigny, shit! You're connected!

Sometimes Meddlesome, now Amanda, brought up an old topic.

Don't you wonder about your bio parents? Might explain lots, like why you don't have a girlfriend or why you still have a landline.

I wonder, but what if they both work for Roto Rooter? I'd rather not know.

That's called avoidance. What if your dad is a nobel prize winner?

I hear you but am just letting it go for now. John Keats—the poet, you know—said it's better to live in mystery. Maybe I like not knowing who I am, staying an enigma.

But don't you wanna know what diseases you carry? Like Huntington's or Hodgkin's or Addison's or Graves' or Crohn's or Barlow's or crab lice . . .

Slow down. Crab lice isn't an inheritable disease.

Jess knew this was once again a dodge. He *was* curious.

As he turned more and more to cyberspace, Jess found his world-elsewhere episodes more frequent and intense. As their chat became more intimate, he found himself texting Amanda about his alter ego, Fergus, and the adventures he was having without even trying, the many women who yielded to the power of his eyebrows. Fergus had the self-possession not to brag. No, as a courtesy to Fergus, Jess would not divulge his last name.

Sometimes Jess would enter into a trance of sexual opportunity as he chatted with Amanda. He sensed it was a dark compensatory aspect of his personality. Maybe he, for all his mild manners, was as much a predator as ordinary jerks. In his mind's eye, Fergus would seduce Amanda, turning the power ratio around, eliciting her curiosity and passion.

Whenever he snapped out of it, he was ashamed of himself and the immortal word trail he left behind. He worried she might call his bluff. *Let me meet him!* she might insist. *Let me have him, just once!* And then what would he do? He couldn't deliver anything other than a phantom, a wishful aspect of himself.

Meanwhile, neither Jess nor Amanda pushed toward meeting one another. Cyberspace was enough, for now. And Jess worried about those twenty-six new lovers a year Amanda was taking via nerve.com. If he got attached to her, he'd be jealous of a single new lover. Multiply by twenty-six and that way madness lay.

Among the many reasons for his feeling befuddled these days was the slow retransformation of Gilah. When he saw her during Natalia's dining excursions, he'd silently register the changes. That exquisitely wrought fusion nose was slowly enlarging and developing a subtle hook. The right cheekbone continued to sag and the chin to recede—not to the extent of being once again weak but still without the authority of a Joan Crawford. And— could it be his imagination?—he noted a slight elongation of the entire face, if not to equine proportions. Here he could keep a clear conscience, since the facial shortening had been the work of Dr. Levy.

It had been almost two years when Natalia again sought an audience with him, this time at his office. With Nurse Prindle out of earshot, she asked if he had noticed any dramatic changes in Gilah.

"Even supermodels get older," he replied. "Remember Lauren Hutton. She keeps going despite the diastema—you know, the gap in her front teeth—and some new wrinkles. Down the line there's always the promise of a routine face-lift."

"That's not what I mean. The entire shape of Gilah's face seems to be shifting. It's hard to spell out."

"Has she noticed anything different about herself?"

"We haven't discussed it. But she spends more time primping in the bathroom and her agent hasn't been calling. She hasn't been on Page Six more than once a month lately." Natalia paused. "And there's something else."

"Oh?"

"Her infidelities. While her face has been changing, she's been stepping up the pace."

"How do you know?"

Natalia looked at her hands abjectly. "Well, I've been stalking her, hate to admit it. Yes, tables turned. But I can't just jump to conclusions."

"And what have you concluded?"

Deep sigh. "Sumalee was just for starters. I'd park near her apartment on Mercer Street when Gilah said she was having drinks with fashion reps and, sure enough, the two of them would arrive arm in arm. I'd just sit there for two or three hours, sick with jealousy . . . and aroused. I wondered if Gilah was the top, what they were saying to each other. I knew which apartment was Sumalee's, and I'd wait for the lights to go out, then it seemed like forever and the lights went back on. Then Gilah would leave alone and catch a cab. I'd try to beat the cabbie back to Bethune Street."

"That's taking a big risk in this town, trying to beat a cabbie. You could break your neck. It shows how much you care. I'm sorry, Nattie, I'm really sorry about all this." He really was.

"She must have been showering at Sumalee's after they finished, maybe together—there'd be a scent of jasmine. Those evenings she was overly attentive at dinner—compensating? But afterward we rarely made love. She was tired and preoccupied. These days I hear her talking in her sleep—in the adjoining bedroom, we don't share a bed anymore. But I can't quite make out the words. Sumalee is history now, thank God, but I'm sure there are others right now, under my nose."

"Gotta ask why."

"Well, new female names have been appearing every month in her address book. I jot them down and do Google searches. They mostly live in the area and do all sorts of professional things that have nothing to do with cosmetics and modeling—grooms, spiritual healers, CEOs. She's out many evenings and doesn't tell me where or with whom. I'd look through her email if I had the chance. Haven't figured out her password."

"Well, what do you think all this means? The changes and all."

"It's obvious, isn't it, Jess? I'll try to put it all together just for you. As Irma Frumkin she was shunned by everybody, even at Bronx Community. I became the great exception when she seduced me at Ophelia's, but I shunned her afterwards and she began stalking me and changed her name to Margaret Epstein. And she changed her past. Jewish aristocracy of Miami, Smith College—who was she kidding? Well, you, of course. Then you made her into a work of art, Gilah de Champigny. That went to her head—she's only human. She loved me during those long years of being shunned and I loved her, but I hid it from myself—I couldn't believe I was in love with a woman and such a homely one. The love came out that Halloween in 1995. It was enough for a time."

"Then what happened?"

"I'm not a great psychologist. Just like you. But all these identity changes—I think she's forgotten who she is. There's no Gilah there anymore. She's just a reflection. And now the reflection is changing, no longer perfect, even weird-looking, and she's desperate—she's hoping she's still Gilah de Champigny and is out to prove it."

She lifted palms up and shrugged, as if to ask what was she to do. "You know, I liked it better when she was Irma Frumkin."

"I don't mean to rub it in, but you said long ago you never get jealous."

"That was then. You're right, now I'm jealous as hell. It's awful, I'm going nuts." Nurse Prindle shoved open the door to tell Natalia her time was up.

Over the next few weeks Jess found it more and more difficult to elude sudden trances during surgery. Thank God for Nurse Prindle, who would intervene with a pig's bladder filled with dried peas attached to a long stick. She bopped him over the head and he would come to. She got the idea from *Gulliver's Travels* and found the item itself on the website of Museum of Useful Things.

Keeping up with Horace had become a labor in itself. His friend called him daily about his new gay life. What a difference a transformed body made! He'd meet men in places like the Manhole on Ninth Avenue or the Monster on Grove Street, but he claimed successes with women too. Since Horace was a lawyer, Jess didn't know how much to believe but didn't challenge his friend's stories. Horace said it was still Sergei, the mendacious prick-tease, who was the center of his erotic life.

Jess thought about Gilah, Amanda, and Horace. All were relentlessly promiscuous, though styles and motives differed. In no case did their behavior seem to have much to do with sex drive or pleasure. He sensed it was owing to deficits of one kind or another, and he found himself worrying about these people who by chance had come into his orbit.

Life out of wedlock, in Natalia's reassigned sense of not being married, wasn't easy.

At the same time he envied their extravagance. He wondered again if he was getting his share of life's feast. Maybe he should have more adventures, let things happen, explore unknown ground.

One crisp Saturday morning in the spring of 2004, Horace called to propose a day in Central Park. He wanted to walk his dog, Christo, a petit basset griffon vendéen who had just reached puberty. Horace expressed concern over Jess's recent moodiness and a reticence about what was bothering him.

"It's nothing, Horace. Just the blahs."

Jess wasn't constrained by a stapled stomach, so Horace loaded up on picnic fare at the Jefferson Market. When he saw the stuffed backpack, Jess feared his friend had gone overboard. But with his new set of muscles, Horace was primed to serve as porter so long as Jess held the dog leash.

This proved no simple matter, for as soon as they left the Grand Army Plaza and headed toward the Serpentine Pond, Christo, a hairy sausage on short legs, set off in pursuit of all moving things, dragging Jess along. He was improbably hung for a mutt, and any creature possessed of living DNA fueled this source of public embarrassment. Jess wanted to whisper to everybody, "This isn't my dog." Christo felt like a concretized life force rippling energy to Jess through the taut undulating leash.

"You are some dog, Christo!" said Jess, as Christo wrapped his front legs around a large red-eared slider turtle caught off guard and began humping.

"Say, Horace, maybe I should take the backpack and you deal with your dog. I can't pull him off this turtle."

"He isn't bi—he's poly. We should all be as open-minded."

As soon as the stressed turtle escaped into the water, diving to a depth beyond the sexual predator, Jess managed to tether Christo to a wrought-iron bench where the two hominids sat and stared westward at the Hallett Nature Sanctuary. In pre-park days, the sanctuary was called Pigtown after its immigrant squatters, long since evicted to give way to what were considered by city officials to be higher-end species, such as birds.

Horace and Jess were graced with a white egret who alighted at the water's edge and stood in magisterial profile, a supermodel among birds.

"I wish to ask you about Gilah," said Horace, opening the backpack and uncorking a split of Veuve Clicquot in plain brown wrapper. "Have you by chance noticed something odd? She simply doesn't seem like the Gilah we thought we knew—she's eating twice as much and sounds fairly manic—arrives late for our dinners and leaves early, lame excuses about her agent, her board of directors . . . She appears to make Nattie unhappy—have you noticed?" He handed the split to Jess and looked for the beluga and toasties.

Jess didn't wish to betray Natalia's confidences, and this wasn't some bloopy chat room in cyberspace, so he didn't fill Horace in. "Everybody gets older, especially supermodels."

"But there's something about her looks," persisted Horace. "It's not just age. Jess, between you and me, her face seems to be falling apart!"

Not knowing Jess was the fabricator of that face, Horace wasn't aware of his faux pas.

"Hadn't really noticed." Jess swigged the champagne while thinking this wasn't a great kickoff to a walk in the park.

"You're a plastic surgeon. Could you possibly undertake a modest face-lift? Of course it'd be awkward to broach the matter, but I truly care about Gilah and would hate to see her undone."

"I wish plastic surgery were magic. It isn't. Let's go to the zoo."

But the zoo was off limits to pets, and Horace knew he couldn't pass Christo off as a seeing-eye dog. Christo didn't seem interested in the zoo anyway and pulled them up the path across Gapstow Bridge, past the Wollman Rink and the Dairy, intent, it seemed, on the Carousel. In the 1870s a merry-go-round on the same spot was run by a horse and blind mule. The present structure was an advance in engineering and featured fifty-eight magnificent hand-carved horses. Pets were allowed on the carousel as long as owners held on to them in one of the chariots. With difficulty Christo was constrained to a chariot, for he wished to hump a horse. "They're not real, Christo!" shouted Horace.

What's real? Jess had had trouble with this question his entire life and found himself in a profession that specialized in fakery. And now he was pondering whether he was gay. As the calliope music and movement began, he questioned his own motives for being there with a gay man. Wasn't he giving tacit encouragement to an elaborate daylong seduction? Did he want this to happen? And wasn't Horace entitled to the fruits of his labor?

The carousel accelerated and the rush of peripheral objects was making Jess dizzy. He steadied his gaze by looking at the handsome man sitting in the chariot with a horny dog. No, he couldn't say he felt any itch, but the idea didn't seem out of the question.

"What do you hear from Sergei these days?" he asked a while later, as Christo dragged them in the direction of the mall.

"Everyday something new. He's very bad, you know, stealing twenty identities by now. I should report him, but he's got me by the you-know-whats and he knows it. It gives him a charge to confess all to a lawyer."

At the entrance to the mall they passed statues of Sir Walter Scott and Robert Burns. "Burns said something about, if only we could see ourselves as others see us, we'd . . . well, we'd kill ourselves."

"Was that his conclusion? Surprising, coming from you, Horace. Three years ago you might have killed yourself, knowing what you looked like to others. Instead you took measures and now you're a hunk. Isn't this a victory of willpower and medical intervention?"

They ambled down the promenade beneath the stately elms as squirrels headed for cover at the approach of Christo.

"Up to a point, but I confess I'm still unhappy. In a sense I did it for Sergei, and where has it got me?"

"I read *Death in Venice* and the *Symposium* and—what was it?—*Civilization and Its Discontents* as an undergrad. They all say the same thing—desire means wanting, and wanting means not having, and not having means never getting—that last one's the kicker. But I'm not sure it follows."

Horace nodded toward the Naumburg Bandshell. "Mick Jagger said we can't get any satisfaction. I only hope he's wrong."

"Okay, but just to pursue this, Sergei *means* precisely what you'll never get. And that's why you'll always need him. If you had him, you wouldn't need him."

"That's almost as good as Oprah. But it's a dark way of looking at desire."

Christo bolted after a nearby border collie who had for a moment escaped her owner, and the two of them circled feverishly around Jess, wrapping him about the knees with two leashes.

"Now that's desire," said Jess, trying to untangle himself. "Some German philosopher says desire is 'life's intensity,' it's not just *not having*. Look at your dog, that's gusto in living. Problem is, he makes trouble for everybody else."

Christo dragged them across the terrace and down to Bethesda Fountain, where the bronzed Angel of the Waters has presided over everything from Victorian ladies in corsets to skinny-dipping potheads to Korean wedding parties. One of the latter, a common sight on Saturdays, was posing for the camera, and it was with difficulty that Jess restrained Christo from humping the bride and, failing that, the groom.

"Back to Burns," said Jess. "He's all wet. Seems to me that we don't see others any better than we see ourselves—we're rotten at both. That's why the camera is such a drag—we didn't know we looked like that, but we also didn't know our friends and lovers looked like that until the camera pegged them. And you're talking to a plastic surgeon. Maybe it's not our fault, because what is there to see in the first place? Sergei has twenty-one identities now, if you include his own and my arithmetic is right."

"Ah, Sergei! Ah, humanity!"

They beheld the lake, with dozens of boaters and swans competing for space, and the Loeb Boathouse to their right. They thought of grabbing a martini, but Christo had a different idea and lugged them along Navy Hill, across Bow Bridge, to the foothills of the Ramble. He must have nosed it out because the Ramble is the densest woodland in all of New York City, with many creatures worth chasing. You've got birds of spring—warblers, kingbirds, heron, tanagers, and grosbeaks. You've got mammals— groundhogs, raccoons, squirrels, chipmunks, and feral cats. And you've got gays.

Yes, the labyrinth of woodland paths in the Ramble had long been a habitat for gay assignation. As Christo towed them up one path and down another, barking, salivating, and humping, they spied men standing alone in postures that signaled receptivity to strangers. Since Horace came forearmed with a man, it would be carrying coals to Newcastle to undertake a seduction where so much gay sex was already going on. And too trite. So Jess figured he was safe if they unloaded the backpack and had their picnic here.

They found a secluded grove near the small pond at the center of the Ramble, with protective shadbush and viburnum, blooming crabapple trees overhead, and the scent of azaleas and lilacs. Not a bad place for a checkered tablecloth and the over-the-top spread that Horace began laying out. With a stapled stomach, he would eat vicariously.

The foodstuffs put Jess in mind of Natalia. "You worry about Gilah, I worry about Nattie," he said. "Those Zagat guides have really cut into her trade. People no longer want detailed culinary narrative, they want a few numbers that tell them if the food and service are good, and if the check will give them heartburn. And she's lost the fight against fusion food, you know. We have some of it right here." He pointed to the Mediterranean spinach salad confused with scallop tempura.

"That was the closest she's ever come to a moral cause, as far as I know," said Horace with a sarcasm that befitted a lawyer speaking of ethics.

"Oh come on, you underestimate her. Remember she protested the 2000 election, worked the soup kitchens at Ground Zero for weeks, marched with the rest of us to stop the Iraqi invasion . . . and she really cares for Gilah."

Horace opened a full bottle of Veuve Clicquot this time, produced crystal goblets, Deruta ceramics, and sterling cutlery, and began serving up fois gras de Strasbourg, guacamole, quiche de Georges de Fessenheim, cold lamb chops à l'anglaise, a noble Stilton, champagne grapes, four kinds of Swiss bitter chocolate, and a joint. Jess didn't have the heart to tell him that what he really wanted was meatloaf on rye with Gulden's mustard. Still, he ate and drank zealously, soon feeling tipsy from the champagne. Horace took a few cautious nibbles.

"Yes, she cares for Gilah," he said. "And, Jess, how shall I say this? You probably know what I wish to say . . . I really care for you."

Jess looked away. Throughout the picnic Christo, tied to a crabapple tree, had been yapping and struggling to get free. "Let me take Christo some of this guacamole," he said, getting up and then thinking better. "I mean lamb chop." The chop turned the yaps into slobbery chomps for a time, an improvement of sorts. Jess sat back down, embarrassed at being a prick-tease and chickenshit. Horace was trying so hard. *Why am I resisting?* Jess wondered. He'd taken no loyalty oath to het-sex.

"You've been working hard keeping that dog inbounds," said Horace. "Kindly permit me to give you a back rub."

Jess said nothing and Horace set to work on his shoulders as Jess sat facing away from the ravenous dog. He had to admit it felt good. Horace had taken no classes in anatomy but seemed to know his way around the muscle groups, probably from clocking hours in the gym. As the massage went on and Horace began working muscles closer to his butt, Jess drank more champagne and breathed in the pot his friend was now smoking. He had noticed that the Ramble sometimes smelled more like a bar in Tijuana than an arboretum. A few minutes passed. Then the odd sensation of a shaved cheek pressed against his ear, and he wondered how women tolerated his own stubble. He didn't much like the aftershave. He was about to say something when . . .

A man with the large proboscis appeared from behind a gnarled olive tree, rather out of place in Central Park, and announced that Jess was to be inducted into the Greek sodality, and he would feast at a banquet of initiation. "Young aspirant, step inside the vestry and allow me to introduce the boys. But first, as your longtime mentor I should formally reintroduce myself. This evening I am Agathon and this is my taverna, where the octopus surpasses what one finds at Tavern on the Green." A group of men in sandals were lying on their sides and plucking grapes. "And around the slab behold Phaedrus and Pausanias, and what's your name? . . . Oh, Eryximachus, sorry, but

with a name like that, what do you expect? And there's Aristophanes,
he's quite the joker. That gorgeous hunk in the military uniform is
Alkibiades, and there in the corner, unaware of anything I'm saying,
stands an unbathed wretch with a wart who goes by the name of
Socrates. When he's not in a trance, he's a clever fellow, fast with a
comeback. We're hoping for a visit later on from Diotima, a drag
queen. Now could you please slip out of those Levis and wrap this
towel around your waist? You'll find a free jockstrap at the portal."

Jess knew he was in a trance—it was like knowing you're in a
dream and being powerless to get out—but he had read Plato's
Symposium and this wasn't quite how he remembered it.

"Sorry, Agathon," said Jess, "but I've got a prior engagement—
with, uh, Artemis."

Agathon frowned but didn't block his escape.

Jess staggered out of the taverna into the awaiting arms of
Horace, who seemed unaware that his friend had been in another
world. Jess was relieved that they were both still fully clothed.

"Sorry, Horace, this just isn't for me. Sorry, sorry, sorry."

Horace took it well enough. Jess threw another chop to Christo,
who was marking territory with a vengeance.

"Please don't worry. I'm used to rejection. Not just Sergei—
many a rejection when I was still fat. Now I have a little more luck,
but not always. I was truly attracted to you, but I can see it will not
work. Shall we simply go back to what we had?"

"I hope it's no blow to your self-esteem. You're an attractive
man and very eloquent. I just . . . don't seem to swing that way."

"Thanks. This helps."

"By the way, I don't mean to pry, but you said you've had some
success with women?"

"Some, but in reality I don't swing that way either . . . I
exaggerated. There was only one woman—a couple of months ago.
She sought me out, never made clear how she came across my name,
but did she ever know how to win her way into a gay guy's pants!
We did it only twice, and she said the second was our farewell fuck.

Might I tell you that I was much relieved. Was quite wary about going down a different path, just like you. And she seemed to have satisfied whatever interest she had in me. But she had pluck, and if any woman could have converted me, she was it."

"She spoke of a farewell fuck? Horace, if you don't mind my asking, what's her name?"

Horace hesitated, as behooves a lawyer, then replied, "Her name was Amanda . . . Amanda Morley."

— Chapter Ten —

AT THE CLUB

"How's Vincent treating you these days?" asked Jess over his landline. They had sunk to the human voice.

"She's my alter ego," replied Amanda. "I eat, drink, and sleep Vincent. I lie where she lay, I dream her dreams, I'm taking up smoking and serious drinking, I'm never having children. My favorite Vincent lines—'I shall forget you presently, my dear, / So make the most of this, your little day.' That's my motto for living. It will head up one of my how-to chapters."

"But I thought she got married."

"Yeah, to a widower named Eugen Jan Boissevain. He never locked her in. He nursed her when she was ill—which was, like, all the time. He supported her career and bought her an island and told her to have affairs with younger men. She was really depressed when he died."

"And romance in *your* life these days?"

"Got a hookup tonight. I'm meeting him at the Knickerbocker in an hour, if you wanna spy." She'd told him early on that she was an exhibitionist. But Jess hesitated to take her up on these offers. "His name is Moxie and I'll know him by the retro ducktail and three-day growth. He writes screenplays."

"Who doesn't? Sounds like a two-nighter to me."

"You never know. I'll tell you all about it."

Jess and Amanda had carried on for months without meeting. She told him what she looked like—petite and skinny, hair so dense and curly it looked Afro, large brown eyes, a slightly crooked mouth. She'd been a preemie and felt her features were not quite finished and her profile embryonic.

As in his personals, Jess described himself to her in modest terms—fairly bland features, feeble eyebrows, hair a darkish brown that used to be auburn and thick but was now showing the extent to which Rogaine doesn't work, hardly fat but without any remarkable musculature. A clerk at Duane Reade once told him, though, that he looked like D. H. Lawrence.

"D. H. Lawrence, shit!"

"It's a stretch, Amanda. Lawrence had strong eyebrows."

She already had a fair idea of what he'd looked like years earlier when he was in the society pages escorting Gilah. As a teenager she read all kinds of trash. But he confessed that time's winged chariot was taking its toll in his early forties. And no, he didn't have a way with women, never had.

His friend Fergus was another matter, he would say, as he drifted into one of his trances at night. He would be sipping Polish potato vodka, and the rhythms of Amanda's speech were hypnotic. He would forget for the moment that he was making everything up. "Yes, Fergus did a 2:53 marathon without training . . . The one in Hartford, not the city. His work is in New England. He's here only for conferences and parties . . . Yes, he's managed to stay unmarried but gets lots of offers—from both sexes . . . No, not macho . . . Yes, some women have told me what it's like to be with him—they always mention his eyebrows . . . How could I introduce you when we haven't even introduced ourselves? . . . No, I'm not going to tell you his last name."

Sometimes they had old-fashioned phone sex and Amanda, more aggressive than Natalia, would say, "Be Fergus, use his voice, tell me what you want!"

"If I were Fergus I'd begin by rubbing your shoulders from behind and then I'd, uh, kiss your left ear."

"No, *be* Fergus, don't just pretend. No conditional tenses!"

Jess fashioned Fergus stories using an antiquated gourmet sex manual—ice cubes on the belly and flirtatious pillow fights. But Amanda could tell whenever he was just reading aloud. "Stop that, Jess! Make it up!" Knowing her exhibitionist itch, he would create a crowd to watch whenever she deployed what she called "attack fucking." One time the scene was the Greek and Roman installation at the Metropolitan Museum where patrons gathered around in evening gowns and tuxedos and applauded when Amanda and Fergus stepped up their pace toward a mighty finale on a cushioned pedestal next to the winged sphinx.

In return she gave him detailed and mildly satiric accounts of her hookups, telling him who was interesting, dull, fat, or lean, who was sexy, who was a bummer. Jess knew there had long been something about him that encouraged people to tell him their amours—was it that he wasn't particularly judgmental? With Amanda he felt both eagerness and a special dread whenever she told her stories. Partly it was because the two of them had not yet met and the mind's theater was all they had. How easily might it disappear! And against his early resolve, he gained an attachment to Amanda, whose promiscuities made those of Catherine the Great look like Chastity herself. He felt her life was different in kind from the sexual revolution of the sixties and seventies—the faded era that codgers and old ladies were still carrying on about.

* * *

One day in late 2004, Gilah made an appointment at his office, requesting a full hour. The secretary would have been eager to oblige a couple of years earlier, but with Gilah's star fading, she was reluctant to give her Dr. Freeman "for the hour." And then there was the nurse to deal with.

"Please, Miss Prindle, leave us alone for a while," requested the doctor.

Nurse Prindle cast a cold eye on the two of them as she stepped out and slammed the door.

"Jess, we've got to discuss a couple of things. I've not confronted you about this before . . . we're friends, but what's going on? My face is falling apart."

Jess drew a deep breath. Yes, it was reassuring to clients, as well as persuasive to juries, to deploy jargon, so he gave it a try.

"Let me examine you closely, Gilah," he said, as he put on his magnifying visor. "Yes, I see there's been a slight reversion within the ostia and bony relationships of the facial bones, as well as a certain compromise of the extraocular muscles resulting in some relaxation of adjacent structures, as well as a malar flattening that is not infrequently one of the regrettable sequelae to this type of implant, and then I see some shift of Merrifield's Z angle in your menton."

"Jess, are you fucking telling me that I'm fucking going to end up looking like my old fucking self?"

"Well, not exactly. But you know that's what most of my clients request anyway!" He tried to laugh at his little joke. She sat there. "We could undertake some revisions, but it would be a long haul once again, and no guarantees. Very sorry about this, Gilah." He was. There was silence for a minute.

"No. I've had a good run as Gilah de Champigny. I might as well become Irma Frumkin again. Nattie says she liked my old horsy face, so if it doesn't bother her, it doesn't bother me. Breathe easy, I'm not going to sue. Thanks to you and Tom, I'm already rich. Anyway, Jess, I didn't come to complain about my silly face. There's something else that's bothering me lots more."

"No, Miss Prindle, we're not finished! Please close the door . . . Now, Gilah, what's bothering you more?"

"It's Nattie. I'd like your advice. You know her as well as anybody." She was wringing her hands. "It's upsetting, but I've learned she's straying."

Jess hadn't let on, of course, that Nattie had told him of Gilah's own indiscretions, beginning with Sumalee and ending nobody knew where or whether.

"Sorry to hear this, and surprised," said Jess. "But what makes you believe it? Remember, Othello jumped to conclusions."

"Not a handkerchief, it's the usual culprit. She left her email open. Couldn't stop myself, I opened some and came across one that I read and reread and reread, torturing myself. I remember every word. 'Had so much fun with you last night, Nattie. Can we do that all over again sometime soon? I loved the way you touched me, loved the feel of your plush bod against my bony bod, loved how you tugged on my Afro. These words are for you: "Faithless am I save to love's self alone. Were you not lovely I would leave you now. After the feet of beauty fly my own." Please don't run, Nattie, let me catch you again on wings of song.' That was it, word for word. She didn't sign off and the sender line didn't give a clue. I heard Nattie coming up the stairs before I could open others. What do I do, Jess? I'm so jealous I want to kill myself."

"Well, I wouldn't confront her. Just know that whoever this is, she doesn't hold a candle to you. Has Nattie cooled on you?" Jess was doing his best as a friend to ask the right questions.

"No, if anything she's been hotter this last week than in a long time. But maybe it's because she's thinking about this hottie while she makes love to me."

Jess thought maybe so but said. "Gilah, this is hurting you, but it's just a momentary lapse, I'm sure of it. You haven't stepped out on her, I assume . . ." He was being a sneak.

"Well, don't tell her but yeah, there have been some lapses, but they didn't mean anything. I was just shoring up my self-image or some such horseshit. Nattie's the one I love."

"I think maybe don't say or do anything for the time being—just pour on the affection. If I know Nattie, she'll break it off. My hunch is it was just a one-night stand—well, maybe two nights."

"Thanks. I'll try to keep my trap shut. But I'm afraid I'll make a scene and let her know that I know."

"By the way, one thing I don't know for sure is who wrote those lines of verse she stuck into the middle. Do you?"

"Oh Jess, even people with no education know those lines. They're Edna St. Vincent Millay!"

The interview ended when Nurse Prindle pounded on the door telling them time was up. After Gilah left, Jess ran through his mind what he knew that others didn't—and it was getting confusing. He would have to keep focused not to spill beans in all directions. He wondered if he should confront Amanda, who had so far seduced two of his intimate friends, but he decided to monitor her quietly. For one thing, he wasn't sure what her motives were. This was targeted seduction, not the casual liaisons of nerve.com. Why was she targeting his friends? Shouldn't he be outraged? But just as when Margaret used him to get at Nattie, he felt oddly flattered. Maybe this was Amanda's way of getting at *him*. Still, should he be protecting his friends from this predator? Well, not really. They were consenting grownups and able to protect themselves. Horace had suffered no permanent damage. And Jess knew Amanda well enough to predict she'd move on after one more encounter with Nattie for old times' sake. Maybe it was even a plus for Gilah to be reminded how much she cared for Nattie.

In any event, here was a novelistic complication in his fairly pedestrian life, and he might as well see how it played out. If matters got serious—if the relationship of Nattie and Gilah were truly endangered and Amanda persisted—he would urge her to lay off.

And Jess wondered what it was like to have literal sex with Amanda instead of just fantasy. He had not asked Horace, thinking this would only encourage a gay connection. But he hoped that Natalia would be forthcoming and confess the affair, giving him the details. So far he knew only Amanda's side of things—what she did and felt in bed with other people. Natalia's erotic connection with her made him desire both of them all the more.

They reverted to text messaging.

Befuddled: *What are you up to, girl? I have two rhinoplasties, one blepharoplasty, and half an otoplasty.*

Meddlesome: *Half?*

Befuddled: *The lower half is fine. You?*

Meddlesome: *The gym, teaching my seminar, working on Vincent, and tonight going to the fuck club.*

Befuddled: *Fuck club?*

Meddlesome: *I've got a hookup. Le Trapeze. No guys or girls alone, no gays or lesbians, just straight or bisexual swingers, and no booze or drugs. BYO condoms and Astroglide. A hundred fifty bucks per couple. Includes veal cutlets and shooters—a real bargain for this town.*

Befuddled: *Swinging couples only? So Victorian!*

Meddlesome: *The joint is uptight. The women touch each other but the men are homophobic. My new girlfriend was pissed I couldn't bring her. Wanted to put on a guy disguise and try out the food.*

Befuddled: *New girlfriend?*

Meddlesome: *I'll tell you about her sometime.*

Befuddled: *All ears.*

Meddlesome: *I could hide a walkie-talkie in my hair and take you with me. They'll never know.*

This time Jess signed on, and the prospect interfered with the day's rhinoplasties and the blepharoplasty, not botched but not up to standard. He canceled the otoplasty out of sympathy for his middleweight client. *What would boxers do*, he wondered, *if they knew what went on in the minds of their plastic surgeons?*

Pinned close to her left ear, the tiny walkie-talkie enabled Jess and Amanda to converse as she approached Le Trapeze at 9:00 p.m. and hooked up with her hookup. Tonight's date was Eric, an adjunct assistant professor of sociology at Baruch who had told her he was less interested in sex than sociology. He'd be taking notes for a peer-reviewed article.

"I'm Amanda. You're pretty cute. Every time I come here it's different. Just relax, let's have some fun."

"You're ten minutes late. I see that the staff here is Mexican, probably illegal immigrants. Do they behave as servants or play an active role?"

"Like servants in Victorian households. They look straight ahead and serve up towels. Servants . . . hey, are you, like, into submission?"

"Yes, I submit articles to *Sociology Today* and other journals, but few takers, I'm only an adjunct."

"Then you must be used to rejection. There's a code here—you don't have to do anything with anybody if you don't wanna. People don't wanna get their feelings hurt. You just move on to the next couple. Maybe they'll play with us."

Jess was listening keenly, but so far it wasn't any sexier than his lab work in vivisection.

"Here's where we undress, Eric. We share a locker, they bring the towels, we wrap them around our waists. Makes for some guesswork." Jess heard the swishing of garments sliding off. "Holy shit! I didn't know sociologists had muscles."

"Are you by any chance anorexic? Don't get me wrong, Elaine—"

"Amanda."

"Yes, well, you're hot, but boy are you skinny!"

There was some static and Jess couldn't make out a reply. Then he heard Amanda again. "Here's the main room. We take any mattress by ourselves or get with another couple . . . Look at this crowd—Thursdays have discounts for seniors." Jess heard background noise that put him in mind of shuffleboard. "Let's sit here. We can get a good look at people going to the upstairs rooms just in case we wanna follow them."

Jess overheard Eric speaking to what he could only guess were people on a nearby mattress. "I see that you are engaged in male superior sexual congress. That's a dated practice. Are you here by chance because of the Senior Discount Plan?"

"Get lost, meathead."

Amanda intervened. "Eric, go easy. Don't ask questions like that."

Jess could hear another couple approach and make introductions. Judd was a certified public accountant from Jersey City, Judy was his secretary, and they were here to play. Amanda whispered, "Eric, you do her left, I'll do her right." Some female moans. *Too theatrical*, thought Jess.

Then, "Ouch! Judd—sorry, I don't do anal at this club. No hard feelings."

"I thought anything goes. Your numbers don't add up, dorks. Judy, let's find the real swingers."

A moment later, Jess overheard a woman's outburst. "I saw that! You liked it. I'm going to kill you!"

There were rapid footsteps and Eric screeched.

"Lady, you just stepped on my boyfriend's toe," said Amanda. "Nobody wears stilettos in a fuck club. God, Eric, you're bleeding!"

An observer chimed in. "Lady, a fuck club ain't the place for jealous shitfits."

"That's nasty, Eric. Here's some Kleenex. Uh, you getting enough sociology?"

"Ample."

There seemed a shift of gears. From what Jess could hear, Amanda was cutting through sociology to the chase. "Eric, why don't we do it ourselves just a bit. Don't come too soon, the evening's young."

Jess heard lots of encouragement from Amanda, if no words from the wounded sociologist. "That's good, really good. Look, they're watching!"

A minute passed. "Sorry," Eric said. "Guess I'm tired."

"Not a problem. It happens. Let's take a breather."

"It would seem," said Eric after the breather, "that most of the people here are over fifty and well above two hundred and fifty pounds, the men that is. Seem to have hired help—low-end female escorts from the Yellow Pages—and they're not fulfilling their contracts. A high percentage of the elderly are unable to achieve erections, let alone sustain them, though I'm one to talk. I commend the escorts for trying, but the whole scene looks like something out of *The Last Days of Pompeii*."

"Eric, you're so smart! But look over in that corner. An exception?"

"Yes, they appear to be under fifty and don't take up so much space on the mattress."

"Come on, let's go have some fun."

Jess heard some scuffling across the orgy floor. "Hi, I'm Amanda. This is Eric. Don't mind the blood. Are you guys new to the club?"

"First time," replied the male, deep-voiced and resonant.

"You guys stand out, with all these fatsos here," said Amanda. "First time I've been here on Seniors Night. You wanna play with us?"

"Just this once . . ." said a female voice. "Don't get hooked on my boyfriend!"

Jess whispered in Amanda's ear. "Be as descriptive as possible. I want to feel I'm there with you."

"Did you hear something?" said Eric.

"Be cool," said Amanda. "Okay, guys, I'm verbal, all right? I wanna give a running account. There's something about you. It's . . . your eyebrows!"

"I like yours too," replied the gent. "They're thick and chocolate brown."

"Hold this, Eric," said Amanda, presumably handing him her towel. "I gotta skip the preliminaries."

Jess heard orgasmic gasps—it seems Amanda was astride the stranger. "My God! This is the best I've ever had. Sorry, Jess, I mean Eric, but shit!"

Eric said, "This is a tough act to follow, Elaine. Would you mind if I were to retrieve my notepad?"

"Remember, just this once," said the woman, her voice shrill. "We're not giving you any names or addresses. He's mine."

"Okay, he's yours," said Amanda. Then in a whisper, "But can you just tell me your first name? You're sooo fucking good."

There was a pause. Then the man replied, "Fergus. My name is Fergus."

Chapter Eleven

THE RECOGNITIONS

Horace had dispatched an intern for the wait-all-day-in-line ordeal to get free tickets to Shakespeare in the Park, and on a warm evening in late May 2005, with their reversion to simple man dates mutually understood, he and Jess returned to Central Park for a production of *Twelfth Night* at the Delacorte Theater. After dinner outdoors at Tavern on the Green—where the enchanting Japanese lanterns and Pom Pom Paradiso martinis made up for the squishy rigatoni alla rustica and tough-as-nails seafood fra diavolo—they found their way to seats in the open-air amphitheater.

"Ouch! Are those stilettos, mister?"

"Sorry about that," Jess said. "Say, are you by chance the famed sculptor, Sinead Macantsaoiel?"

"*Feared* is more like it," said the woman's companion. "People fear pronouncing her name. You did well."

"I have a knack for Celtic names, and I never forget a face. That was quite a write-up you got in *Art News*, Miss Macantsaoiel." Jess had upgraded his office magazine shelf and was having plenty of downtime after *New York Magazine* included his name among "Worst Plastic Surgeons in New York."

Sinead Macantsaoiel smiled and introduced her companion, Bentley Harvester.

"I'm Jess Freeman and this is my friend Horace."

"Jess Freeman," Sinead said. "That name's familiar. Did I read about you somewhere recently?"

Horace intervened. "*Twelfth Night* is my favorite Shakespeare play. I was forced to learn the Duke's opening speech in eighth grade. Had no idea what he was talking about but I still remember the lines: 'If music be the food of love, play on. Give me excess of it, that, surfeiting, the appetite may sicken, and so die.' It would be difficult to say it better, would you not agree?"

"Do you understand the lines now?" asked Bentley.

Jess went into a sudden brown study as the other three continued their get-acquainted chatter. Yes, he understood the lines all too well by now. An excess of love had aroused and then sickened his appetite, but for better or worse it wasn't fully dead. After his vicarious evening with Amanda at Le Trapeze a few months earlier, he felt such intense and perplexing sensations that once again he retreated. Already in cyberspace, he tried to remove himself further by hovering above it all, telling Amanda he needed to withdraw from Eros altogether and could they please not communicate for a spell? She agreed.

"Take your time, Jess, but please, pretty please give me Fergus's last name? I'll still be yours." Of course he couldn't give it because he didn't know it. This sudden materialization of his phantom alter ego was an existential eruption of imagination into real life. It inflamed him and festered. He sought the wise mentor who appeared again and again in his trances. Surely he would know how to cure the nausea brought on by Fergus having sex with his cyberpal. Where was he?

After a few weeks, he simmered down, and Amanda and he resumed their mutual cyberspace interrogation. He kept jealousy at bay by reminding himself that vicarious sex was better than no sex at all. He couldn't be sure how Amanda felt about him—and frankly he wasn't sure how humans of her generation felt their feelings. But at least she was attentive and seemed to remember everything he said and wrote.

Not carrying a pig's bladder on a stick, Horace pinched him in the ribs to bring him back into the conversation just as he was about to enter a trance. "Bentley just asked you what you do, Jess."

"Very little. I'm a plastic surgeon."

"Oh, now I remember, faintly," said Sinead, looking down at her hands.

At opposite ends of the foursome but leaning across their companions, Bentley and Horace were hitting it off.

"Most of Shakespeare's sonnets were written to a beautiful youth, not the Dark Lady, you know," said Bentley.

"Yes, even 'Let me not to the marriage of true minds admit impediments.'"

They somehow shifted the topic to the evolution of the gay community in Chelsea, then back to Shakespeare, his unhappy marriage, and the second-best bed he willed his wife. Jess and Sinead exchanged knowing glances.

The performance was splendid and all four wept at the reunion of the twins, Viola and Sebastian. The clown sang his song—

But when I came, alas! to wive,
With hey, ho, the wind and the rain,
By swaggering could I never thrive,
For the rain it raineth every day

—and Bentley suggested nightcaps at the Boathouse. The misty lake there was illuminated by a gibbous moon, and two radiant swans swam close to the shoreline.

Bentley told them he acted at the Pearl Theatre, a company on St. Marks that specialized in classic repertory. He was best known for his portrayal of the villainous Count Cenci in Percy Shelley's play. At a festive dinner party, the count jubilantly announces the deaths of his two sons, one through an act of God when a church falls on top of him. "This is a real downer for the guests, who were looking forward to dessert," chuckled Bentley. "And it's a good prep for the incestuous rape I'm about to inflict on my daughter Beatrice. 'Can anybody be this bad?' friends ask me when they read the script. But I like impossible roles."

In his late forties, Bentley looked the part of an actor, with dashing silver hair, a Byronic purple silk shirt, and a throaty bravura of speech.

Jess guessed that Sinead was a fairly young forty. She kept an apartment in Westbeth, the artists' housing complex only a few blocks west on Bank Street and close to Natalia's townhouse. She was supported by the Dia Art Foundation and had a country house near Cooperstown where she spent summers. He was surprised he had never run into her in the Village.

"I was married for a time to a philosopher. What a mistake! I keep him in a large hope chest in my upstate studio. I nailed it shut so he can't get out."

"If he's a philosopher, he can turn inward," offered Jess. "I try it whenever I'm slapped with a malpractice suit."

The couples tacitly agreed that everybody should get together again. But they soon paired off—Horace began dating Bentley, and Jess began dating Sinead. Feeling by now more relaxed about communication with Horace, Jess and he swapped notes on their progress, which in both cases was slow to get physical. Horace and Jess agreed they were serious in their own intentions, but each was anxious about his date's reluctance. Was the erotic current that drives romance anywhere to be found?

Jess also shared more than was wise with Amanda, whom he still hadn't met.

"What's she look like?" she asked, on her cell from the bar at Five Points on Great Jones Street.

"Not bad. A little plumper than you say you are but not busty. She has long red hair, very dramatic, and green eyes. Creamy complexion. Smiles a lot—that's an unusual trait among the women I've known. A melodious voice. Oh, unlike what you say of yourself, she wears lipstick . . . No, we haven't even kissed yet."

"You must be eager." She sounded testy.

"Less eager than anxious. I'm not sure she finds me attractive."

"Where's she from? What's her story?"

"I don't know all that much yet. She grew up in Portland, raised by adoptive parents, went to Reed College, studied sculpture at the Royal Academy in London. She was married to a philosopher she keeps in a box, no kids, shows her work at Dia Chelsea and lots of Dia venues outside the city. Her Westbeth loft is like a fantasy—high ceilings, interior balconies, tapestries, nude sculpture—that's her specialty. Tropical birds fly around and squawk like hell. Sometimes they poop on the sculpture."

"Has she asked you to model?"

"No, but she does men more than women, old and young, buff and fat. Guess I'd be eligible. Would you mind?"

"Just remember, Jess. I'm your girl. You got that?"

Over the next few weeks into early fall, Jess and Sinead continued dating, still going slow. Jess himself felt some hesitation he couldn't account for. But they were companionable and did many New Yorkish things—the Circle Line, shooting billiards at Corner's on Fourth Avenue, watching Bentley play Cyrano at the Pearl Theatre, and eating rice pudding at a Mafia joint on Spring Street. They disclosed relatively little of an intimate nature about their lives up to now.

The match was encouraged by Natalia and Irma, who had expressed some regret to Jess over deceiving and dumping him. *Irma* was once again her name, not Margaret or Gilah. They hoped he would find a real match. Frequently, they invited the new couple to the Bethune townhouse, eager to convince Sinead of Jess's worth by the quality of company he kept and their great fondness for him. They all hit it off. Of course they didn't tell Sinead about his earlier involvement with the two of them.

But one evening she said, "They seem eager to convince me of your worth by the quality of the company you keep. And their great fondness for you is always in my face. A compensation? Jess, you must have had unhappy affairs with them both."

He admitted it, hoping this would not be the end. But it seemed to make Sinead only more interested. A keener psychologist than Natalia, Irma wondered aloud to Jess if the attraction between Sinead and him had some grounding in narcissism. They had so much in common, from their having been put up for adoption to their fondness for pine nuts.

Watching this new relationship develop seemed to remind Natalia and Irma of the value of their own. Each tacitly reaffirmed her commitment to the other—and as each told Jess—were managing to forsake all others. Fully accepting that she was no longer glam Gilah, Irma had nothing to prove and stopped sleeping around. She let her lustrous red hair—much like Sinead's—revert to mousy brown. She changed her perfume from L'Heure back to Jicky.

Having successfully seduced Natalia, Amanda lifted her siege, removing any temptation to stray, but Natalia was herself no longer vulnerable, now that Gilah—aka Irma—wasn't sleeping around. And contrary to the modern practice of letting it all hang out, Natalia and Irma never went through an exhaustive confessional coda. Apparently it was enough for each to have told Jess of the yellow bile. When the mutual roving stopped, so did the suspicion and jealousy. Each silently forgave the other, and their life together resumed its earlier rituals. Irma was once again the top, Natalia the bottom. And since Irma was no longer a supermodel, cassoulet was reinstated on Natalia's menu.

For his part, Jess never confronted Amanda regarding her seductions of Natalia and Horace. It wasn't just to avoid a scene. He silently remained flattered that Amanda had been making love to him from a distance by means more literal than talking and texting. For a time he kept her posted on Sinead and their courtship, which still did not include any sex. For her part, Amanda kept up the interrogation, still on the phone.

"Did you choose a dark corner last night? Did she eat the lamb chops with her fingers? Did you share the crème brûlée?" Jess could hear more evidence of jealousy in Amanda, even as she continued her own amours unabated.

"Went to the fuck club last night with some nerve.com worm named Henri. Bummer sex, and no Fergus in sight. Come on, Jess, what's his last name?"

"How's the work going on Vincent?"

"I'm writing the chapter on how to keep your self-esteem in a relationship where your lover cheats on you. Vincent was good at it—the cheating part, that is."

Then, as Amanda seemed to fear, it happened. Sinead asked Jess if he would mind posing for her—she wished to do a Prometheus. The liver-eating vulture would not be portrayed, only the suffering Titan. It was a tough pose because he would be recumbent but twisted. No, he didn't need to look agonized all the time and, yes, he could wear a jockstrap.

Jess considered not passing this plan along to Amanda, but it seemed to violate their implicit contract of total transparency not to, and it wasn't as if she were keeping some monogamy vow of her own. Anyway, it was for the sake of art, not romance.

"Don't tell me nothing's going to happen," said Amanda. "Remember you and Gilah—it's just like that. Sinead can't look at your bod for hours and not get ideas, and you're eager to strut your stuff."

"You've never even seen my stuff. Maybe romance would fizzle."

"So it *is* romance—you admit that much."

"So far no *Casablanca*. I'm beginning to think you care, Amanda. Could it be that *you* are jealous? I'm delighted!"

She was quiet on the line.

Then Jess said, "Is this some new kind of double standard? Seems to me you've done some flitting about on your own."

No response again and Jess knew he'd overstepped.

"Okay, Jess, I'm irrational and unfair and yeah, it's a new double standard. You guys have imposed on us for centuries. Now it's our turn. So yeah, I don't want you to have sex with that woman. If you do, I'm outta here!"

"But you and I have never had sex, at least not in person."

"Boy are you befuddled! Can't you see how much you mean to me? You're just about the only person I *don't* have sex with! Obviously I love you!"

This vaguely reminded him of Natalia's peculiar ways of defining sexual meaning. He was bemused and a little touched.

He didn't call off the sittings with Sinead. But he felt an odd guilt about them and had to remind himself that many observers would say he was entirely within his rights to pose and also to seek a real live girl. "I'm under no obligation, no obligation, no obligation to Amanda," he'd say to himself like a mantra.

He didn't want to lose her altogether, so—as with Natalia when Margaret Epstein entered the picture—he opted for secrecy. He would stop giving her such full reports on his comings and goings with Sinead.

He began push-ups during downtime in his office, much to the consternation of Nurse Prindle. He asked Horace where online he might obtain a more flattering jockstrap.

The sittings began and Sinead worked slowly. At this stage she was making only a life-sized maquette in clay of the larger-than-life cast bronze for which she wouldn't need Jess at hand. The Dia Art Foundation was paying for everything, including vintage Hoffritz steak knives, which Sinead used to incise a swirly surface. Jess was, as usual, anxious even in the midst of promise, so it wasn't hard for him to take on the composure of someone whose liver gets eaten every day.

"One thing I like about working with your body, Jess, it's middle-aged and a little flaccid. I need this because I'm confronting centuries of an idealized Prometheus."

"As I recall, Prometheus wasn't middle-aged, he was ten thousand years old and not at all flaccid. Quite something that a geezer chained to a rock could tend to his pecs while waiting around for a vulture to eat out his liver. For the Greeks the liver was the organ of desire, you know."

"Please don't talk so much right now, Jess. I need to focus on your body. Give it more torque. Move your torso ever so slightly to the left and raise the right arm an inch or two. There, that's good—hold that. And keep quiet."

So the evening sessions went. From time to time, through the normal patterns of penile flush and flow, Jess would suffer an incipient erection. But Sinead never made mention. He figured she had spent hundreds of hours with male models more naked than he.

During moments when he was permitted to relax his pose, they would talk. He told her more about his early years, and she told him more about growing up in Portland. It had never occurred to her not to be an artist. Her father was a professor of English at Reed with a passion for Irish studies, and her mother an organizer of arts-and-crafts fairs. They were anti-Vietnam, pro-free-love types. Both had encouraged Sinead to be whatever she wanted—it was called *self-realization* in those antique days. When she showed an early knack for making clay vessel flutes that sold at craft fairs, she was on her way to a major career. Jess could not but feel some envy that his string of foster parents had not been equally supportive of his little figurines and wooden effigies.

No, she didn't know anything about her biological parents, nor did her adoptive parents, who had filled out some forms at an interstate adoption agency and lucked out. Jess felt there was something intrinsically likable about Sinead. Whatever the usual hard knocks of her growing up in tempestuous times—and a mysterious period she mentioned in passing when she was hospitalized as a teen for a dissociative mental disorder—she had a certain buoyancy and optimism about life. Also a generosity that could get her in trouble, when, for example, she overestimated her philosopher boyfriend's flexibility and expansiveness of soul. It seems she projected qualities onto him not possessed, as she discovered only after they married. He had in fact the soul of a woodchuck.

Sinead had resisted the tides of fashion in the sculptural art world—minimalism, pop, conceptualism, realism, and the like—though she admired environmental earthwork from afar as she went about her own unabashed and intense figurative sculpture, gaining a devoted following and receiving a glowing review from Roberta Smith.

She was often quoting Percy Shelley, and Jess, reading the poet on his own, came across an astonishing passage in "A Defence of Poetry": "The great secret of morals is Love; or a going out of our own nature, and an identification of ourselves with the beautiful which exists in thought, action, or person, not our own . . . The great instrument of moral good is the imagination."

Jess sensed some goodness in Sinead that had its ground in her imagination, which, Shelley notwithstanding, has been the source of intolerable mischief as well. The Crusades were a product of the theological imagination, responsible for centuries of sieges, starvation, flayings, and beheadings. He and Sinead were, in their way, pagans—and Prometheus seemed a fitting subject for their cooperative effort.

It was the evening of the final sitting, a Thursday in mid-September. "Are you chilly, Jess? Put on this robe while I mix the clay." She was wearing a green long-sleeved turtleneck beneath broad plaid suspenders that held up messy blue corduroys.

She spoke of *Prometheus Unbound*. "You know, Jess, Shelley's great melodrama has these sisters, Asia and Panthea. Asia is engaged to Prometheus but it's Panthea who has the erotic dreams about him and shares them with her sister. 'I saw not—heard not—moved not—only felt his presence flow and mingle through my blood till it became his life and his grew mine and I was thus absorbed.' I think those are the most erotic lines ever written."

"So Asia wasn't jealous, wasn't afraid Panthea would run off with her man?"

"No, Panthea made it all possible, helped Asia float in her drunken boat toward Prometheus and rescue him with love. Don't you think that's beautiful?"

"Yes, it's beautiful, but I'm convinced that jealousy is King, even in the age of cybersex when everybody is supposed to be free-floating and nobody gets jealous. Was there a Greek god of jealousy? There should have been. From my coursework in evolutionary biology, I know you can't rewire a sexually possessive animal with a new set of cultural premises. It takes more than a decade to change two hundred thousand years of trying to shut out the other guy's sperm."

"Jess, this is what I like about you. You sound smart sometimes—really smart. But the most jealous of the Greeks was a goddess, Hera, Zeus's wife. She gets jealous, then she gives *him* good reason to be jealous. She fools around behind his back."

Then she put aside her mallet and declared the maquette done. Together they looked at it in silence. *Yes*, thought Jess, *it is a middle-aged body with fairly loose musculature, but what Sinead has wrought sums up the pluck and suffering of my entire life.*

It was both magisterial and intimate, honest and embarrassing. It was the ancient Titan brought into the sphere of human realism, where and only where he could retain some meaning.

Jess saw that she had removed his jockstrap and rendered his parts with a decently accurate guess. She had saved this for the last.

"Maybe now we could," she said, and they shared their first kiss. A minute later they were throwing off clothes and heading for a divan on an interior balcony. Lying beneath her, he kissed her shoulders and left ear, and they pressed lips together.

"I love you, Jess."

"I love you, Sinead."

Rolling over, Jess was just about to enter her naked body the old-fashioned way, her loosening thighs welcoming him at last, when there were shouts at the door and pounding. It sounded as if someone was warning them to flee for their lives. Sinead grabbed her corduroys and top and ran for the door while Jess looked around frantically for his jockstrap.

Sinead flung the door open. "What's up?"

There stood a striking young woman, very thin with large brown eyes, a slightly crooked mouth, and a wild bush of stringy black hair. "Jess Freeman and Sinead Macantsaoiel, I have to tell you that the two of you . . ."

"The two of us?"

"That the two of you are . . ." She bit her lower lip. Then she smiled wryly.

"The two of us are what? Get on with it," insisted Sinead.

"I have to tell you that *the two of you are twins!*"

Chapter Twelve

ROOTS

After Jess awkwardly introduced Sinead to someone he had never met—"She's a kind of pen pal"—they sat around the kitchen table and Amanda told them of her cyberspace journey to the truth.

"I was trying to find out about you, Sinead, and I turned up stuff you obviously don't know."

"But why were you interested?"

"Because I'm in love with your twin brother. Is that all right?" Some sarcasm here. "I wanted to know about my rival." Jess squirmed.

"But you two only just met!"

"You're showing your age, Sinead. The younger generation falls in love in ways you've never thought of."

"Jess, are you in love with Amanda?"

Jess squirmed some more. "Well, I'm quite *fond* of her in a digital sort of way. But I thought I was in *love* with you." He averted his eyes from Amanda, who frowned.

"And I thought I was in love with you. Now it seems we're twins. Does that mean we're no longer in love?"

"Not sure . . . Maybe we should hear the evidence. Amanda, why are you so sure we're twins?" he asked.

Amanda looked into the eyes of her rival. "With a name like Sinead Macantsaoiel, you were a sitting duck for identity theft. And once I stole your identity, the rest was easy."

"You stole her identity?"

"Your friend Horace's cock-tease, Sergei, told me how. I seduced him a few weeks ago and he told me all about it in bed. It was like taking lessons from a grandmaster. He swore me to secrecy about his methods."

"Why did you go to the trouble of seducing Sergei?" asked Jess, vexed.

"No trouble, it took maybe half an hour. Be flattered. It's 'cause he's in your daisy chain—just not a major daisy."

Sinead was sitting forward and glaring. "How dare you steal my identity! Give it back, bitch. What have you done with it?"

"I had my reasons. Jess told me you were raised in Portland by adoptive parents, so I posed as Sinead Macantaoiel seeking my biological parents and did a little nosing around in interstate records. In, like, twenty minutes I discovered that the agency was in Albuquerque. Your adoptive father was getting one of those useless degrees, a master's in English at the University of New Mexico."

"Yes, that much is right."

"Once I found the agency, I sent them a letter demanding the identity of my biological parents. They refused, but then, with a little help from the Children and Youth Department—I threatened to sue. That changed their mind. They faxed me the names of your parents and mentioned a twin baby boy complete with specs—everything from the color of his eyes to that birthmark you say you've got on your butt, Jess. By the way, didn't it seem fucked up that you two share a birthday?"

"We do? What's your birthday, Sinead?"

"May 1, 1962."

"My God!" he exclaimed. "Yes, that's my birthday. It's just about the only thing I know for sure. I thought it unpolitic to ask about yours. I was never told I had a twin."

"Me neither," said Sinead.

Jess reflected that it should have been obvious all along, but two first-rate minds can miss the obvious if, on some level, they wish to ignore it. This was bad news.

"So are you guys at all curious about your bio parents?"

"Yes, yes! Tell us!"

"Your mom's name is Emer Kenny. Your dad is Tyrone Mullen."

"Does that mean I really am Irish?" asked Sinead with warmth.

"Irish Protestant on your father's side, Irish Catholic on your mother's," said Amanda. "Not my place to comment, but that sucks. Like waging a holy war in the living room. They live in a log cabin a few miles north of Taos, close to the Colorado border. I've got their address, if you want it."

"Shouldn't we have been adopted together?" asked Sinead.

"Like a twofer? Your adoptive parents were living in a dirt-poor hut on Lead Avenue in Albuquerque. People with a master's in English are lucky to have room for one kid, let alone two. After that, Jess, you had no takers for three years, so they dumped you into the foster-care system."

"I can't believe they did that," Sinead said faintly.

"It's all in your records. When you guys were up for adoption, it was, like, a buyer's market, except the buyer got paid. Until a lawsuit was filed in 1980 and not settled until this year before Judge John Edwards Conway—got that?—children in foster care were, like, nomads. They camped out in one foster home after another with parents who were collecting stipends and to hell with adoption. Your first were the Freemans, Jess, those ghost-town hippies, and later it seems you were living in a teepee. What I don't know is why your bio parents put you up for adoption in the first place."

There was silence around the kitchen table. "Well, sis," said Jess, "she knows too much to be wrong. And why *did* our parents dump us?"

Sinead took the question, walked across the studio and stared a long time at her maquette of Prometheus, then turned abruptly and said, "No sense living with an enigma. Pack your bag, bro, we're heading out to Lobo mountain!"

* * *

Two days later, after a red-eye flight, Jess and Sinead were driving a rental Jeep Cherokee out of the Albuquerque airport and up Highway 14, the Turquoise Trail, toward Santa Fe. It had been almost three decades since Jess had seen the landscape of his youth. Passing by the Sandia Mountains and through the village of Golden, site of the nation's first gold rush in 1825, they reached Madrid. There, some things remained unchanged. A few time-warp hippies of the sixties were in evidence, still smoking weed on porches and wearing beads and saris, changed only in wrinkles, jowls, and frowns. The twins stopped at the company row house where Jess had lived with his first set of foster parents. Same old shack of decrepit wood planks. Nobody home. Elsewhere the town was gussied up. An old train-engine repair shop had been converted into an opera house, and the Mine Shaft Tavern requested reservations.

Then on to Cerrillos, where the business façades were those leftover Western movie sets, and the dirt streets still had more dogs than people.

"Thomas Wolfe wrote a novel about this sort of thing. *You Can't Go Home Again*. Never read it, the title says it all."

"Are you sure you were really here in the first place?" asked Sinead. "Isn't this what we Irish know so well? We go home to a place we've never been."

"Too metaphysical for me."

Jess was anxious and melancholy. After the adrenaline of discovering the identity and whereabouts of their birth parents, both he and Sinead were having ups and downs—one minute full of expectancy, but the next grumpy because incest cast a wet blanket on their love affair and they feared they might tell their folks to go fuck themselves. For the first time he admitted to himself some real anger at the desertion and wondered how their parents might try to exculpate themselves. Maybe the anger had been lurking there all along.

Amanda had equipped Jess with a voice-activated two-way digital pen spy recorder that she placed in his shirt pocket. On this adventure she wanted to overhear *him* and have some input along the way. Sinead reluctantly conceded they might need Amanda's ready services as a digital geek. Others in Jess's circle—Nattie and Irma, Horace and Bentley—insisted they be kept informed, and Amanda would serve as conduit.

As they were reaching higher elevation, the jeep lost power for lack of oxygen. Jess remembered that outsiders sometimes suffer altitude sickness in Santa Fe, and now, oddly, he too was an outsider. Yet he felt nostalgic when the scent of juniper pines sweetened the air. And approaching the outskirts, he said again and again to Sinead, "This doesn't belong here, *that* doesn't belong there!"

For most of its history, Santa Fe had no outskirts. It was all old town. Now it was indistinguishable from Skokie. The Villa Linda was a shopping mall so immense it couldn't be stuffed into Chaco Canyon. And, wait a minute, was that an Arby's? And a Burger King, a Blimpie, a Baskin-Robbins? And there was Denny's, the International House of Pancakes, Wendy's, Long John Silver's, Kentucky Fried Chicken, more than one McDonald's, more than one Taco Bell—all just on Cerrillos Road coming into town! He hoped he was hallucinating from the thin air, but no, Sinead confirmed the sprawl.

"Come on, you're overreacting, Jess. The heart of the town will still be there."

"Yeah, come to think of it, Prometheus held on to his heart while the vulture was eating his liver." He was so distracted by his sense of non–déjà vu that he almost rear-ended a Mercedes SL. "Speaking of eating," he continued, "we need to pick up something before hitting the road to Taos."

They grabbed a couple of Big Macs and were on their way. Getting through town was no easy matter because this was the time of the annual fiesta and everybody was in town for the ritual burning of Zozobra, the giant effigy. Amanda checked in on her cell to advise them of the best detours. She called again to say that, acting as their travel agent, she was unable to book anything in Taos but there was a recent cancellation at the famed Inn of the Turquoise Bear on Buena Vista Street. She directed them there.

The sprawling adobe inn had impressive rock terraces, huge pines, a flower garden, and a deep-backed *portal*. Jess hurried in alone. The clerk, an elderly man in Western attire and turquoise string tie, greeted him. "Yes, Mr. Freeman and, uh, companion, we just heard from your travel agent. You're in luck, a last-minute cancellation. You'll be staying in the Edna Millay Room."

"Whose room?" asked Jess, startled.

"You're from New York and you don't know the famed poetess of Greenwich Village? She was here in 1926. The owner was Witter Bynner—he proposed to Edna in 1919, she said yes, then he took it back because he was gay. They stayed friends. This place was known for gay-lesbian soirees in those days, and we're still gay-lesbian friendly."

He winked and took Jess's credit card. "Never heard of Edna St. Vincent Millay. *Tsk.* You've probably not heard of D. H. Lawrence—he stayed here in 1922, his first night in New Mexico. Hmmm, anybody ever say you look a little like him? Except the eyebrows."

"D. H. Lawrence I know about, never read him," said Jess. Informing the clerk that they'd return late that night, he and Sinead sped on their way, passing the Santa Fe Opera, Tesuque Pueblo, and the village of Chimayo, famed for its *santuario*. There, thirty thousand people annually on Good Friday are cured of all diseases. The magical Sangre de Cristo Mountains on their right seemed to say that, yes, this *is* the Land of Enchantment, but nothing could slow the Jeep Cherokee as Jess and Sinead gunned their way north to uncover their roots.

Like Santa Fe, Taos was bumper to bumper and Amanda once again gave up-to-the-minute traffic information. They barged past Kit Carson Park and took Route 522 to San Cristobal. From there they followed signs to Lobo mountain and passed others telling them they were heading toward the D. H. Lawrence Ranch.

"Forgot to mention, D. H. Lawrence stayed in our hotel in 1922."

"D. H. Lawrence, wow! I learned everything I know about sex from *Lady Chatterley's Lover*," said Sinead.

"I never found out what you know about sex," he groused. "We had a close call."

Turning onto a deeply rutted dirt and gravel road with a Dead End sign, they continued their ascent. It was late in the day and sunlight cast long shadows through the cottonwoods and aspens. The air was thick with the scent of resin. Jess felt they were going back in time to an aboriginal grove of fragrant, gesturing trees— until they encountered head-on a van full of people and negotiated the road.

"You guys making the pilgrimage?" asked the scruffy driver, a massive elbow protruding.

"Well, it's *a* pilgrimage, I suppose. You must be speaking of D. H. Lawrence."

"You're going to be too late to get into the shrine but don't worry. What a joke!" Laughter from everybody in the van.

They weren't going all the way to the shrine anyway. After another half-mile of road rut, they came to a rusty mailbox that faintly read, Kenny/Mullen.

"We're here," muttered Jess. "Now what?"

Jess's cell vibrated and Amanda spoke. "Gotta tell you guys that what I'm getting from dot.org adoption sites is that, like, it's not a good idea to sneak up on your birth parents. You should write them first and arrange for a phone conversation where you sound each other out. They have their feelings and their rights too, you know."

"*Now* you tell us!" said Sinead.

Amanda continued, "Your parents might not even be home, did that ever occur to you?"

"The lights are on," said Jess. "We're just going to sit here a minute and catch our breath."

"I've been in research mode," said Amanda. "Your elevation is 8,151 feet and you're looking at a four-room homesteader's cabin made of aspen vigas and adobe. If you turn around you'll see the desert and the mountains of Colorado. The D. H. Lawrence Ranch is just a mile up the way. The people who owned this place before your parents get into Lawrence biographies. It's a small daisy chain of a world, Sinead. I was introduced to sex by D. H. Lawrence."

"I'd rather not hear about it," said Sinead.

"By the way, Irma and Nattie and Horace and Bentley are all here rooting for you," said Amanda. "We're at the Internet Café. Activate your spy camera. We'll be watching and listening."

Their friends cheered them on. "Don't trance out now, Jess!" "Stay focused, Sinead!"

"Thank God this can happen only once in a lifetime," said Jess. "I see somebody moving around in there."

"Okay," said Sinead, "take a deep breath and let's go knock on the door."

As they approached the weather-beaten porch bestrewn with chewed-up bones and cracked earthen jars, they could hear shouting and what sounded like kitchenware clanging. A puppy was growling and yapping. They couldn't tell if it were taking sides or just joining in.

"Maybe we should come back tomorrow," whispered Jess.

"Don't we want to know who our parents really are? What better way than when they're fighting?"

Sinead knocked with both fists so as to be heard over the din. The human voices quieted, the puppy kept yapping. They could hear a man's muffled voice. "Must be those goddam Seventh-day Adventists. Put down the skillet, Em. I'll tell them to bugger off."

The door was flung open and a young bull terrier ran out barking and nipping. "I told you lunatics we don't want any. We're pagans. Take a walk! . . . Oh, you're not the same folks. Bibbles, lay off! Sorry about that. Who the devil are you?"

Jess stared at a man his own height who looked exactly like him except for a beard, some bruises, and twenty-five years. The man stared back, his eyes widening. Jess felt weak in the knees, and Sinead put an arm around his waist as the two confronted their father.

"Mr. Mullen," she said quietly, "I'm Sinead and this is Jess. We are your children."

Mr. Mullen shook his head. "Say that again?"

"We are your children, I'm your son and this is your daughter. We're twins."

Mr. Mullen turned around and shouted to the back room. "Em, come back out. These strangers say they're our children!"

"Sure, they're our children and *you* are Zozobra," snarled Em, appearing at the inner door, a cigarette dangling from her lower lip. Holding a skillet, she slowly approached them.

"Em, if they are our children, don't you think we should ask them in?"

The last thing Jess remembered before he fainted at the doorstep was the face of this woman. She was comely except for some bruises of her own. It wasn't the fact this was his mother that made him faint. It was something else.

Except for the weathering of a quarter century and the green eyes, he found himself staring with astonishment into the face of Gilah de Champigny.

Chapter Thirteen

THE SUMMER OF '61

Jess awakened to his sister's face as he lay on a wicker couch in the front room. She was holding a rag dipped in Irish whiskey to his nose.

"Where are they?"

"In the kitchen fixing dinner," she whispered. "While you were passed out, they said, sure, they put up twins for adoption in Albuquerque forty-three years ago with a stated preference that the adoptive parents be Irish. I told them you have a birthmark on your butt. This was proof enough for them that we're their kids. Have to say, they're taking it in stride and going about their business. They haven't asked me any personal questions."

Jess sat up and looked around the room while an altercation was going on in the kitchen over how to warm up some stew. Tacked onto the vigas were yellowed photographs of Emer in ballet costume, looking even more like supermodel Gilah de Champigny.

Jess now knew that in shaping a new face of raw flesh and polymers for Margaret/Gilah/Irma, he had recreated, as if bewitched, the face of his own mother whom he hadn't seen since infancy.

The backdrop to some of these photographs was the Metropolitan Opera, others the old Santa Fe Opera before the fire of

1967 when the theater was still open to the elements and distant mountains. An upright piano that looked older than the log cabin itself sat in one corner. Jess could read the title of a piano score to the opera *The Ballad of Baby Doe* and, next to that, Stravinsky's *Oedipus Rex* and *Persephone*. There was a short bookshelf mostly of D. H. Lawrence novels and biographies of J. Robert Oppenheimer. Two straight-backed wooden chairs with painted designs of buffalo, horses, and swans. Otherwise the room was bare.

Bibbles barked that dinner was ready and the four sat down at the pine table in the kitchen. On the table were the stew, a bowl of dried figs, a bottle of Bushmill's, and four shot glasses.

"Is this Irish-Southwestern fusion cuisine?" asked Jess, noticing plantains floating about with a rabbit carcass. He was trying to be nice. He heard a groan from the pants pocket where he'd tucked his spy pen—a groan he knew to be Natalia's, as she and the gang continued eavesdropping.

"Ty snares and skins the rabbits, and, yes, we are Irish-Americans and, yes, this is the Southwest," replied Emer. Silence.

Tyrone was dressed in Western attire—two-steppin' boots, Wranglers, an embroidered brown shirt, string tie, and prominent silver belt buckle. Like Jess, slender and unprepossessing, he had brownish-gray hair and an uncoordinated reddish beard, blue eyes, and a pallor that showed he wasn't very well. His high-pitched voice sounded asthmatic, maybe consumptive.

Emer was dressed in a pale-green Greek tunic and long-trailing pink silk scarf. She was barefoot. Her long hair was flaming red like her daughter's, if with some help from henna, and like her and Jess she had green eyes.

"Let's catch up," said Sinead. "Are you curious what your kids have been up to the past four decades?"

Silence, as the parents exchanged frowns across the table. Rather than conclude they didn't give a hoot, Sinead continued, "I can imagine you're both a little apprehensive, so we'll just fill you in. No, we're not Scientologists. We're both doing pretty well."

Sinead began giving them an account of her youth in Portland, the modest circumstances of her adoptive parents, her career in sculpture, her brief marriage to a philosopher, and her life in Greenwich Village. Emer Kenny and Tyrone Mullen nodded politely throughout their daughter's recitation and continued eating stew.

"I'm sure you're wondering if you have any grandchildren."

Silence.

"Well, you don't. Jess and I were united completely by chance just a few months ago. We're already inseparable but we won't be having any children!" She forced a laugh. "Now it's your turn, Jess."

Where to begin? Jess was at a loss. He saw no point in putting a guilt trip on these people, so he edited out his foster parents, scoping forward to his good fortune in getting a scholarship to Harvard and his success as a plastic surgeon. No, unlike Sinead he had never married but was doing some serious dating. At this point he heard buffered cheers in his pocket from Amanda.

"By the way, are you two married?" he asked impulsively.

"Em and I have been giving it some thought," Tyrone replied slowly, tugging at his beard. "I've been more or less in favor . . . Em, would you put out that fuckin' cigarette? We're eating! Goddam it, we're eating!"

His shrieks took Jess and Sinead aback as they awaited retaliation. But Emer took a final drag, put out the cigarette on the floor, and hissed. Tyrone had a violent coughing spell. They each drank a shot of whiskey and quieted down. Jess wondered if shouting, hitting, and hissing were simply their manner of negotiation. He and Sinead exchanged bemused glances.

She broke another silence. "We'd be really grateful if you could tell us something about yourselves—you know, how you met, your lives together, how you ended up here in this, uh, beautiful cabin, that sort of thing."

"Beautiful cabin? Are you kidding?" replied the mother, her deep gravelly voice expressive of rage at the edge. "Ty dragged me to this lean-to. It's part of his D. H. Lawrence trip. Beautiful cabin, crap!"

"D. H. Lawrence trip?" asked Jess.

"He thinks he's D. H. Lawrence. Can you imagine what it's like to live with somebody who thinks he's D. H. Lawrence?"

"Well, D. H. Lawrence was my favorite writer when I was a teenager," said Sinead, hoping to placate both parties.

"That's when Ty first read him. He says D. H. Lawrence taught him everything he knows about sex. Not much, you can be sure."

Tyrone stood up at the table as if to upend the pot of stew onto his companion's tunic. Bibbles snarled and went for his ankle. Jess intervened.

"Tyrone, why don't you and Emer just stay put and let's share another round of whiskey and catch up some more. Sinead here was just asking how you two met."

"Tyrone, Emer? You cretin!" said Tyrone. "We've not even been properly introduced."

"Sorry about that. Uh, Mister Mullen, how did you and, uh, Miss Kenney meet?"

Bibbles went again for Tyrone's ankles. He shook loose the precocious pup. "Bitch! Slut! Bugger off!"—and sat back down. The four resumed their silence. Jess passed the whiskey and everybody swilled another shot. And another. After a few minutes of yet more silence, Tyrone began to speak.

"How we met. How we met." He pulled on his beard, then looked at the ceiling. "You've set me to thinking. It was the summer of '61."

"Yes, the summer of '61," said Emer. All at once she looked wistful.

Tyrone took the Bushmill's, swigged from the bottle, coughed, swigged again, and began speaking words that sounded to Jess long in storage.

"You want to know? Okay, I'll tell you what it was..." Another swig. Then, "At dusk, just as the performances began, I sat on the steps behind the theater and looked west across the arroyos to the Jemez Mountains. Light from Los Alamos twenty-five miles away—it had an aura. It beckoned. For weeks that summer I yearned to cross by foot to the source of the light."

"What were you doing there?" asked Jess, sensing a serious shifting of gears.

"Rehearsal pianist for the Santa Fe Opera. Their greatest season ever. Stravinsky was in residence to conduct *Oedipus Rex* and *Persephone*. Vera Zorina—know the name? Greatest ballerina ever— she was doing Persephone. Paul Hindemith was conducting the American premiere of *News of the Day*. I remember some lyrics about love being a nasty itch and scratching making it even worse. Stravinsky and Hindemith were both runts, who'd have guessed they were titans? They walked around the ranch with the rest of us. What's his name, Douglas Moore was there to oversee *The Ballad of Baby Doe*. And there were singers—my God, what singers! Martial Singher, Judith Raskin—she told us lots of dirty jokes, one about the woman whose rump fell off and the doctor told her it was because she was coming unscrewed."

He suffered a brief paroxysm.

"Donald Gramm, Judith Blegen, they were just getting started. It was the first season that Santa Fe had its own ballet company, borrowed from the Met."

Emer picked up the story, with some bitterness. "That's where I come in, the Santa Fe Opera Ballet. I was their star. Only twenty-one. If Vera Zorina had taken ill, I'd have done Persephone. I prayed for it. God, did I pray! That's when I lost my faith. The bitch never got sick. I rehearsed the part with Ty at the San Juan Ranch where we all stayed, and I dreamt of getting a break and lighting up the house. Dancing on that stage was heaven—the redwood floor was the best in the world, it gave with your step, lifted you up. I was floating and the crew would stop and gaze at me—long red hair, I was so lithe. I'd overhear them saying I was the next Isadora Duncan. Vera Zorina? Who cares? She was merely the greatest ballerina. I was Isadora Duncan! I overheard a stagehand say I was Venus. He stood outside the women's dressing room for a glimpse of my bum—so obvious. I let him see it and pretended I didn't know he was looking."

She fumbled with a fig.

"Was it love at first sight for the two of you?" asked Sinead, respectfully.

"Not for me, can't speak for Ty. I never speak for Ty. You get in lots of trouble if you speak for Ty."

"Em, come on woman, you know full fuckin' well I loved you the moment you walked in the studio. You had the *Persephone* score. You were a vision, a rose, my fuckin' heart's delight. It was hard to read the score and watch you at the same time you did those arabesques, slut. Your robe was high above your knees. So much for all that bullshit about spiritual beauty. I stayed awake nights in my bunk bed rehearsing your body."

"Bunk bed?" asked Jess.

"Rehearsal pianists were just a notch above stagehands," Tyrone told him. "That was the problem, a class difference between me and the hoity-toity ballerina. I had no money and wasn't a great physical specimen. Yeah, I looked like you. Not much taller than Hindemith. That twerp was always getting lost backstage between acts and I'd take him by his flabby elbow like an old lady and point him back to the podium. Being ineligible rankled. As the summer wore on I felt more hopeless. I wanted my own brilliant career—that meant Carnegie and the Gewandhaus and the Concertgebouw and the Grosser Musikvereinssaal—a soloist like Schnabel or Horowitz, temperamental, overpowering. But one day I was rehearsing with Stravinsky and the chorus, and he was beating time like a woodpecker and stopped us in the middle of *Oedipus Rex* and told me to go home and practice my part, and was there a better rehearsal pianist who could fill in? That was a blow, being cussed out and sent packing by Stravinsky. I never recovered."

Jess heard faint whimpers in his pocket—he guessed it was Bentley. "Well, what happened next? Those class barriers must have been burned away."

"Yes, but not before I got into trouble. In late July I went AWOL for a day. Was supposed to be there for a morning rehearsal. I stared off at the distant city lights of Los Alamos, and decided to duck out and hike all the way there, yes, twenty-five miles. The fuckin' Germans call this sort of thing *Sehnsucht*. We'd been doing *The Ballad of Baby Doe*—a great nostalgia trip into the old West, the hills of Colorado. The music was all about vitality in the landscape. I wanted to suck up that landscape like a pagan, see the desert up close. But when I was getting my gear together early morning, something weird happened."

He paused, his eyes radiating a blue fire, and Emer breathed deeply, shaking her head. "Okay, Ty, just tell them." Bibbles barked his agreement.

"I thought I was J. Robert Oppenheimer."

"Beg your pardon?" said Jess.

"You heard me. I thought I was J. Robert Oppenheimer. Look, it makes sense. He headed the Manhattan Project. First saw Santa Fe and Los Alamos the summer of 1922—that's exactly when D. H. Lawrence first saw it. They were both here for their health— Oppenheimer weighed one hundred twenty-five pounds and wanted to get some exercise backpacking. Lawrence, you know, weighed eighty-four pounds when he died, poor fuckin' consumptive. Oppenheimer had the same response as Lawrence, who wrote, 'From the moment I saw the brilliant, proud morning shine high up over the deserts of Santa Fe, something stood still in my soul and I started to attend.' For Lawrence it meant writing more novels, for Oppenheimer it meant making the atom bomb. What's the fuckin' difference?"

"Why did you think you were Oppenheimer?" asked Sinead, empathic and good at probing.

Emer jumped in. "He's sick. The cripple finally got it diagnosed. They call it a psychogenic fugue state. You think you're a totally different person and you travel somewhere or other. It's like sleepwalking. He still suffers from it—or *I* suffer. All at once he thinks he's D. H. Lawrence and wanders off. But I know where to find him. He walks up the road a ways and hunkers down at the shrine. I take the roadster and pick him up—I *mean* pick him up, thank God he's skinny—and bring him back. It's one of our routines."

Jess felt tingles. This sounded like his trances—not quite the same thing but close enough. Yes, this was his father. He heard faint wows of recognition from his pocket.

Tyrone continued his story. "I left the opera ranch at four thirty in the morning with a topographical map but no compass. Why would Oppenheimer need a compass? I had a canteen and some chorizo. A local Chicano working as a stagehand had warned me about bears and mountain lions, lent me a .25 caliber automatic. Said I'd need it for Indians too—I'd be passing by a number of pueblos and they'd try to scalp me. I thanked him but said to myself that J. Robert Oppenheimer would never hurt a fly, let alone shoot an Indian."

Jess suppressed any mention of Hiroshima and let his father ramble on.

"The sun was just breaking as I got into the rhythm of walking up and down one piñon-covered arroyo after another, like waves of earth. Tarantulas and rattlesnakes everywhere, but they scampered off and I couldn't be stopped. For a time the elevation was rising and I passed through ponderosas and aspens. Began descending the river valley toward the Rio Grande. Scrubby pines and tall grasses and large rocks here and there with hieroglyphs. The map said I was entering Bear Canyon and, yeah, there was a cave-like opening with piles of bear dung, so I took a potshot at the shit to let the bears know they should stay indoors. It worked—no bears. Near the riverbank I found deserted mining tracks. It was heading toward noon and I was famished, so I sat on a boulder near the river and ate all the chorizo and drank all the water. Set to thinking how I might cross the Rio Grande."

"You must have made it or you wouldn't be here," said Jess.

"And *you* wouldn't be here!" replied Ty. "Did you say you were bright? . . . The chorizo was almost my last meal. The river didn't look swift or deep, and I didn't see any bridge anywhere and was getting impatient about reaching Los Alamos before dark, so I decided to wade across. Easy going at first. The riverbed was squishy but I made good progress with water up to my waist. Held the pistol high but this upset my balance—I tumbled over, sank out of my depth. The gentle stream was an illusion—it was a torrent of death! I heard the gun go off, was taking water in my lungs.

"I passed out and had a delicious dream—I was in Northern Ireland, in County Fermanagh with its tranquil green lakes—that's where my people came from before the famine. I was strolling down to Lough Erne, the world's most beautiful lake. And then I had a vision of Emer here—she was a hamadryad floating through the trees with her silken scarf trailing and her tunic parted to show her naked body, and I saw her nipples and bum. She was smiling, beckoning. And I was all engorged and just about to enter her sweet body when I woke up in a fuckin' helicopter. I felt cheated to be rescued just then. Those half-wits couldn't understand why I was pissed."

Jess heard gasps in his pocket. He was gasping too—his father's story reminded him of his frustrated joy with Sinead and the deprivations of that canoe trip down the Green River with Alison.

"How were you rescued?" his sister asked.

"Seems my Chicano friend blabbed about my plan, and John Crosby—he was the Opera's general manager—Crosby heard about it and was furious and sent out a helicopter even before I could be reported missing. The medic asked me who I was and I said 'J. Robert Oppenheimer' and he said, 'Yeah, and I'm John D. Rockefeller.'"

Tyrone had another paroxysm and fell forward on the table, splashing stew. Emer ran around and set him up in his chair and wiped off his face. "Zeus, you're losing it."

"It's your fuckin' cigarettes, Em, they're killing me."

"That's quite a story, but you still haven't explained how we got here," said Jess.

This was Emer's cue and, like her life partner, she seemed to shift gears. She poured another shot and her eyes rolled upward as if in a trance of her own.

"Ty's right, I had larger ambitions than a summer romance with a rehearsal pianist. I wasn't looking for romance at all—my career was the thing. Who needs romance if you can do Petipa and Balanchine and have Jacques d'Amboise partner you? But I wasn't well known. I was still emerging. So I put up with Ty's silly worship—thick enough to cut with a chop saw. Have to say, he was only one of many. It's just that I spent more time with him. Rehearsal pianists aren't supposed to be good pianists, you know. They have a knack for sight-reading and keeping the beat. If they try subtleties, they get canned—dancers count on them to be metronomes." She knocked on the table mechanically with her fork, mocking her partner with a smirk. "But I could see that Ty was getting out of hand, trying to be an expressive musician. I had to remind him of his limited role."

"When I played for you, I couldn't help it. Shit, Em, what a bosser you were!"

"Keep quiet. I need to focus ... Ty's near-death experience emboldened him. He began behaving as if every moment were his last. That dream in the Rio Grande meant he was entitled. The next day we were rehearsing an extra gypsy dance they'd thrown into *Carmen*. Oxygen tanks are always on hand for the dancers because of the altitude, and I was helping myself to a breather, and he stood next to me holding the hose and whispered the story you just heard about his hike to Los Alamos, I swear in the same words. Maybe it was just the oxygen high, but the story got to me and I began to ease up.

"Ty had access to the company jeep—they asked mere rehearsal pianists to run last-minute errands into town—you couldn't ask important people. One night he knocked on my door at the ranch and said we should go chase jackrabbits. Said there were dozens up on the mesa and you could chase them around in a jeep. Great sport, everybody did it, and I should put on something warm. His eyes were blazing, hypnotic, and I said yes and took my poncho, and we drove up to the mesa."

She sighed and took another shot of Bushmill's. "It was chilly and the night sky was clear. I looked up from the open jeep, the Milky Way was spread across the sky. You could see the Sangre de Cristo and Jemez Mountains where they blacked out the stars. Ty turned out the headlights and drove slowly. No moon but the stars were bright enough to light up the ground.

"Then he cried, 'There's one!' and I could make out a jackrabbit leaping ahead of us. Ty turned on the headlights and revved the engine. The jackrabbit was doing evasive action—you know how foot soldiers zigzag away from the enemy. But he kept the jeep trained and the jackrabbit just ran and ran over the mesa. I watched his huge springy muscles—more a panther than a rabbit—I felt the force of those muscles as we bore down on the poor bastard. He looked around to see if we were gaining, but Ty was just teasing him—goddam sadist—and then the jackrabbit was slowing down, so Ty stopped and let him go.

"We sat a minute with the lights out and looked at the stars. The force of that rabbit got to me and Ty and I started kissing. I wanted more—so we climbed out of the jeep and I spread the poncho on the sand. He was above me, blocking the starlight. We did it again and again there on the mesa until the sun began to rise over the mountains and we said we'd always love each other . . . And that's why you kids are here tonight."

Silence around the table except for muffled exclamations from Jess's pocket. Then Tyrone, "You think you're eating bunny rabbit? Guess again—why is it so tough?" His laughter set off yet another paroxysm.

Jess felt queasy at the thought of what they had in their bellies. But Sinead had the composure to say something. "That's a great beginning. Edmund the Bastard said it's better not to be conceived between stale marriage sheets. It's better to be out of wedlock. If this is where Jess and I came from, it accounts for lots of things, all the good stuff in us, that is."

Silence. Tyrone and Emer looked drained by their monologues like characters out of Tennessee Williams, sitting back in their chairs, arms drooping. But Sinead pushed on. "What happened then? Bring us up to date."

"My brilliant career," sighed Emer.

"My brilliant career," sighed Tyrone.

"Neither of us wanted kids," she said. "We were both set on careers, we were too young, we didn't talk marriage. But remember this was before Roe v. Wade, so when my period didn't come I couldn't just go and buy an abortion. Mexican abortions were cheap right across the border, but all those stories about coat hangers got to girls. So I went full term after we decided to put the kid up for adoption. Didn't know I was going to have twins and each of them a seven pounder. That's not supposed to happen. Why are you both so scrawny? You creeps wrecked my body and my career!"

"God," said Sinead, "I'm so sorry. We didn't mean to."

"I put on heaps by the second trimester, and it was a terrible delivery, and you guys left me with a prolapsed uterus and a permanent tum. I never recovered and there was no way I'd ever dance with Jacques d'Amboise. I blamed Ty, I blamed you. I kept working at it, but the Met and Santa Fe never asked me back. So I gave up my studio apartment in Manhattan and set up a ballet school for kids in Taos, and that's where I've been ever since."

"But the two of you are still together," said Sinead, trying to be upbeat.

"Yes, in mutual catastrophe, and who else was going to want us? . . . But Ty and I get along in our fashion." She sighed.

"Uh, Mister Mullen, what happened to your career?" asked Jess.

"Already told you. I never recovered from Stravinsky's cussing me out—for a squirt he had a deep voice. I entered all the piano competitions but was never a finalist. For a major career you've got to win a competition. When I practiced in private, my Beethoven was greater than Schnabel's, I swear it, but when I played in those competitions the shadow of Stravinsky fell on me and my hands shook and I lost my way. Crosby fired me the summer of '65 after I set out once again for Los Alamos thinking I was J. Robert Oppenheimer. The only job I could get was with Em—rehearsal pianist for her ballet school. And that's what I did for thirty years. Until she fired me."

"Oh."

"But we have our life here in the mountains with the deer and elk, the bears and wild turkeys and quails and your occasional pronghorn," said Tyrone. "There's a lot of life up here. Bibbles is a young dog. And thanks to his wife, Frieda, DHL's ashes are mixed with concrete up the way. I feel energy coming out of that shrine."

"If they're really his ashes," added Emer. "Frieda may have been fooling everybody ... Yes, Ty and I missed out on our brilliant careers, but we live our lives as we live them. We'll never live apart." Silence. Then, "Ty, why don't you play from the *Persephone* score. I'll dance for our company."

"Wonderful!" exclaimed Sinead and Jess.

They went into the piano room, and Sinead and Jess now understood why it was so bare. This was Emer's dance studio. Stravinsky's shadow descended benevolently now because Tyrone sent forth marvelous sounds from the upright as if it were a Bosendorfer, and Emer, after a hesitation, claimed the space with exquisite movement of arms and torso, her line perfect, her feet bare, her tunic and scarf bore her aloft out of Hades into the light of day. This was Persephone, goddess of the underworld who returns every spring to bring new life to cold earth. Emer's élan and Tyrone's pulse throbbed through their children as they watched in bewilderment and awe.

It was too late for Sinead and Jess to return to Santa Fe, so they bedded down in the studio on the couch and a spindle bed. They held hands across their separate cots. Over protests of Amanda and the others, Jess turned off the spy pen, losing its juice anyway. "It's been a long day, gang, we've got to get some sleep."

Just as they were about to fall asleep, they heard some rustling about in the backroom where Emer and Tyrone were sleeping—or so they thought. Jess worried that it would turn into another altercation and more bruises.

But no. Acoustics in a log cabin don't make for privacy, and they could faintly hear voices.

"Yes, Tyrone, I'm here for you, lying in the tall green grass—it's spring again. Come in, lover!"

"Emer, I'm coming home—love me, fuck me, lovely bitch!"

"Always, lover, always!"

Jess and Sinead squeezed hands, grinned at one another, and couldn't help but listen while the lovemaking in the back room went on and on. They finally fell asleep to dreams of jackrabbits, arroyos, cottonwoods, tall green grasses by the Rio Grande and in Ireland, and the rebirth of spring after a long winter in the very mountains where they'd been conceived. Their dreams were good.

* * *

Arising in the morning, they found Emer and Tyrone asleep, so they left a bread-and-butter note. "Thanks for a wonderful evening and sleepover. It was great to reconnect. Keep the home fires burning, and cheers! Sinead and Jess."

They got into the jeep for the drive back to Santa Fe. It was the day of the annual burning of Zozobra, Old Man Gloom, the highlight of the Santa Fe Fiesta dating to 1712, the oldest traditional celebration in the United States.

They were silent as Sinead took the wheel and Jess slumped to her right in a kind of reverie, not a trance. His study of the sciences had taught him to look for patterns, and now seemed the time to seek them out. Keener observers would have figured them out already. He knew he could be dense about people, but the patterns gradually came into focus. He felt entitled to take a crack at all he had done, all that had happened to him. Like Hercule Poirot he wished to put together the clues, knowing himself deeply implicated in the plot he unraveled, even its most likely suspect. *Step forward, Monsieur Poirot, and help me put it all together*, he thought. These were his musings, more or less.

How illusory our freedom is—the circumstances of our birth, our proclivities and passions, our bodies, identities, and everything that comes our way without our asking! Here he was with his twin sister, like those twin siblings in *Twelfth Night* separated and then brought together by chance—chance that then felt as scripted as Destiny herself. Their powers of sculpting the human form—Sinead with clay and marble, he with literal flesh, scalpel, thread, and a little polymethylmethacrylate—must have been their dual biological inheritance, not something tacked onto their identities down the road. Where he, like Pygmalion, sculpted the face of Irma, unconsciously recreating the face of his long-lost mother, Sinead sculpted him in turn as the suffering Prometheus, not knowing she was giving form to her own brother, who wasn't exactly a Prometheus but had some vultures of his own.

Their sudden recoil from sex, once Amanda handed them the news, had its roots in biology also, the incest taboo.

He thought of Natalia, with her large natural endowments of body and mind. She was never in love, never jealous, and meant to keep it that way, finding men who were ineligible for any deeper claim on her as she pursued her ambitions, insisting on boundaries and rules and ethnic authenticity. Yet beneath her regulated life was an impassioned love she hadn't acknowledged even to herself, one that brought along all the ancient torments of jealousy, insecurity and crazed behavior, as she stalked the woman who had stalked her.

Jess thought of those who hoped to redo themselves and lure others, as Irma learned all things Polish in her bid for Natalia, then had her face and very identity recast in a way Natalia might find irresistible. Horace stripped away all excess fat to win the love of Sergei. Humans try so hard to change who and what they are! Does it work? He himself had given gay sex a try, a bad joke. Same with Horace and het-sex. Nature again sent nurture packing. *What we are, we are*, thought Jess, and he found some consolation in this, though he, a plastic surgeon, was ironically the sought-out modern engineer of personal change. Well, plastic surgeons can also restore . . .

And then there was Amanda, harnessing a new technology to human couplings, the stage manager of this pageant. Amanda brought to light Sinead and Jess's origins and imminent incest, and prompted them to seek out their biological parents. She went with them on their adventures, even as she had earlier invited Jess to accompany her on her own. Finding one's identity means finding roots—a commonplace—but Jess was surprised at how powerfully it would take hold of him, and this was owing to the intervention of Amanda.

She herself seemed unconcerned with roots and embraced the illusion that had taken hold in so many of her generation. The world existed to be skimmed and tasted, especially in human encounters, where adventurism supplanted libido, where cyberspace provided a new way of making love at a distance and keeping that distance, and where people seemed to lack a sexual memory. "I've had hundreds of men and don't remember any of their names," Amanda had told Jess. But she herself became as jealous and possessive as the others. For all her talk and habitation in a detached digital world, she too was held in thrall by nature.

Jess felt there was hope for Amanda, maybe a little out of sync with her peers in her powers of attention, her steady purposeful work—she hadn't entirely given up on books!—and powers of bonding. She was, after all, committed to the small group of people who defined Jess's social life, three of whom she'd seduced as a way of getting closer to him. She had also chanced upon Fergus, finding in reality a phantom of his psychic life. Not a little flattering that she had gone to such lengths to get at him! But he worried about whether it was up to the likes of him to tame the adventurism and corral her to domesticity. This didn't seem like much fun, and maybe he'd get small thanks for it in the end. Would they marry?

He thought of himself. No, he had never known who he was, and still didn't, but the recent revelations were self-recognitions—truths always there but never sought out. He had a strong sense of the uncanny in recent months, entering a world both familiar and strange, as when he beheld with astonishment his mother's face in the cabin door. Emer and Tyrone's story filled him with pathos. Defined early on by their ambitions of music and dance, they had only leftover identities as pianist and dancer, but also a fierce somnolent love.

Identities were not, he sensed, self-contained reservoirs to be filled in by mapped tributaries. No, they were truly fluid, with overflows, waves and turbulence, placid intervals, droughts, invasions of parasitic plants, poisonous rain, and sometimes saving efforts by caring folk. Yet there *was* a continuity that sustained the sense of one's own proper name. He was still somehow that same Jess Freeman playing with figures of body parts in the sand near Santa Fe. He remembered that a ninety-year-old Bertrand Russell said this—he was unaccountably the same person many years removed, he was still that little boy.

Jess had gradually annexed multiple identities—rejected suitor of Alison, plastic surgeon, lover of Natalia Wojciechowski and Irma Frumkin, cyberpal of Amanda Morley, friend of Horace Holliday, twin brother of Sinead Macantsaoiel, and son of Emer Kenny and Tyrone Mullen. He cared for all these people and had, in his stumbling way, tried to help them and do them no harm. In return he found that, like D. H. Lawrence encountering the landscape of New Mexico, they had stumbled too but that, in encountering him, something had stood still in their souls and they started to attend. He sensed they all cared for him in their fashion.

The resentment he had held in his unconscious all these years toward his parents and their desertion had gone up in smoke, for there was nothing to forgive. They had every right and motive to give him and Sinead up, for their goals exceeded domesticity. Instead of resentment, he now felt guilt for having been a seven-pound infant who, along with Sinead, destroyed his mother's career.

His ruminations were interrupted a spell when he told Sinead to slow the fuck down, there was a driver ahead with a Jersey license plate.

He returned to his reverie and thought of his trances and Fergus, his phantom proxy. Hmmm, spontaneous eidetic imagery and psychogenic fugue state—maybe psychologists could find a link. This too might show the power of nature over nurture—maybe Jess was just a sorry chip off the block. Sinead had suffered some kind of dissociative personality disorder in her teens but she didn't wish to talk about it. In any event, he didn't need a psychologist to tell him what he figured out that Halloween night many years ago—he'd been practicing love at a distance, longing after Alison, tolerating Natalia's rules and oppositional sex, making Irma a work of art on the outside but not reaching her inner life, and disappearing into trances whenever reality pressured too much. Checked in his resolve to change his ways, he had then found in Amanda Morley a form of love-at-a-distance squared, where he continued to deploy the phantom Fergus. This Fergus was surely a fracture in his personality, another kind of distance—from himself. He wanted to do better than all this.

He thanked Monsieur Poirot and bade him *adieu*. He turned to his twin sister and gently rubbed her right shoulder.

"I love you, Sinead."

* * *

"You must have partied somewhere all night, Mr. Freeman," said the sly clerk back at the Inn of the Turquoise Bear. "We didn't see you here. Great to be in Santa Fe during the fiesta. Maybe now you and your companion are ready to bring in your luggage, unless, of course, you don't have any." He looked surprised when Sinead appeared.

"Don't worry," said Jess, since the clerk seemed a little down at the prospect of ordinary het-sex on the premises, "we're twins." He wondered how many other people took him for gay.

"Here are your tickets," said the clerk, and Jess said thanks, not knowing what they were. "By the way, you'll be staying next to the Igor Stravinsky Room. May I assume you've heard of Igor Stravinsky?" He chuckled.

They checked into the Edna Millay Room and instantly got a call from Amanda, back in Vincent's own quarters on Bedford Street. She explained that the gang had departed last night, a little pissed that they'd been shut out by Jess and Sinead without even a nighty-night. But they all planned to reconvene later that day for the burning of Zozobra. Amanda had already dealt with scalpers and arranged tickets—a pretty penny, the ceremony had been sold out for weeks. She was in a competition with Natalia as to who could turn up more information on Zozobra—Amanda would surf the internet while Nattie would scout out the Jefferson Market Library.

"Tell me about Vincent's suite," said Amanda. "This is research for my book."

Sinead obligingly described the very suite where maybe, just maybe, Vincent stayed back in 1926. No carved initials anywhere. There were viga ceilings, a kiva fireplace, Saltillo tile floors, and a view of the Old Santa Fe Trail—a trail no more, rather a vista punctuated by Hondas and Mercedes.

"Thanks, Sinead, that's enough. Now why don't you guys clean up and I'll tell you where the action is before Zozobra gets torched. In a word, think Canyon Road."

The Igor Stravinsky Room visitors, of indeterminate sexuality, were having a mid-day gang shower and yucking it up. So Sinead and Jess once again got their ears full. Sinead then vetoed Amanda's Canyon Road itinerary. She had read up on the art scene there—its topless fairies, giant rabbits, bronze grizzlies, and acrylics on Lucite. The very prospect filled the sculptor of Prometheus with gloom. Instead, the siblings ordered in guacamole burritos, drank tequila neat with lime and salt, and took an affectionate siesta in each other's arms. When they awakened, dusk was approaching and it was time to set out for the burning of Zozobra.

They headed on foot for Fort Marcy Park. Jess's cell vibrated and Amanda and Natalia began chiming in with their findings. Natalia felt strongly that the weeklong Santa Fe Fiesta should be expunged from the calendar because it celebrated the triumph of Spanish imperialists over local Pueblo Indians. "De Vargas, a fascist conquistador, credited his 1692 victory to a twenty-nine-inch statue of the Madonna. Another embarrassment to my faith. Let me tell him where he can shove that statue!" Irma chimed in to align herself with the Indian underdogs. "I'll bet there won't be many Indians at the ceremony. Would you drive in all the way from a wretched pueblo to celebrate the defeat of your people?"

Amanda one-upped them. "Gotta tell you that Zozobra is a fake that has nothing to do with the fiesta of 1712. Some local nut named Will Shuster invented him in 1924 to protest the commercialization of the fiesta. Now he's the biggest draw and makes millions for the community."

"So what?" said Bentley. "It makes for good theater. By the way, Horace and I would be much obliged if you were to describe the gay-lesbian scene en route to the ceremony. We're thinking of moving to Santa Fe someday like all our other gay-lesbian friends."

"Will do," replied Jess. "And thanks for the info on Zozobra. But I could have saved you the trouble. Remember I'm a native. I already know it all because I was a Gloomy in 1972. Well, I screwed up. Tell you about it later. I'm putting the spy pen in my front pocket."

As they made their way up Paseo de Peralta to Fort Marcy Park, they saw fewer gays and lesbians than kids dressed as conquistadors, with muslin capes and cheap metallic helmets. They were all shouting, "Burn, Zozo, burn!" and waving plastic swords at imaginary Indians. Entering the park, Jess saw that Zozobra had grown since his own fiasco as a Gloomy.

"He's extraordinary!" exclaimed Sinead. "A work of art!"

There he stood, Old Man Gloom, the world's largest marionette, suspended by a sixty-foot metal pole and twelve-foot crossbar, wearing a red bowtie and cummerbund. The long white skirt revealed him to be a cross-dresser. Wires were attached to his arms and mouth, so when the puppeteers pulled them, he gesticulated grandly to protest his impending execution and opened his grotesque mouth to curse the thousands of happy bloodthirsty people. He was stuffed with explosives, along with shredded paper. The shreddings represented all the year's misfortunes and bad memories—divorce papers, court summonses, tax receipts, doctors' bills, and poison-pen letters.

Jess said, "Come on, Sinead, we have to write our Gloom notes and put them in the Gloom box. It gets put into the giant's body at the last minute." The Gloom notes were brief personal requests that woes be lifted and enemies be disposed of in the coming year. Standing amid thousands, they quickly scribbled on pieces of paper from Sinead's sketchbook.

Jess wrote, *Please take away my world elsewhere and Fergus with it.*

"Who's Fergus?" asked Sinead.

"Tell you later. Now read me yours."

"Nothing doing, bro. It's my business."

Around 9:00 p.m. the execution began as drums beat ominously and mariachi music filled the darkening sky. Out came the robed fire dancers on stilts, brandishing torches. Their mission was to tease Zozobra, coming close to his hem with their firebrands without quite setting him ablaze. Then came the Queen of Gloom in a sensual silver bodysuit, there to prevent the destruction of her big man. She was followed by her helpers, twenty-four young Gloomies dressed in white sheets. There was a fierce competition among local prepubescents to become a Gloomy.

"I was one of those," whispered an agitated Jess to Sinead and the gang. "Problem was, I went into a trance at just the wrong moment. I was the lead Gloomy and it was my finest hour. The Kiwanis Club was going out of the way to give foster children a break. We were all doing our swirly snake dance behind the Queen of Gloom when I looked up Zozobra's skirt and saw a giant cobra dangling there. I froze in my tracks, thinking I should warn him, but before I could scream, the twenty-three other Gloomies piled on, falling like dominoes, and the audience started laughing. The Queen of Gloom was quite put out and I was never a Gloomy again."

"Jess, this story is so sad," said Horace. "It could explain some things about our day in the park."

Then came the dramatic entrance of the Fire Spirit, the executioner who scared away the Queen and the Gloomies and danced around the giant's paper skirt. And like a matador, he probed and taunted his victim, playing proudly to the audience, which began chanting "Burn him! Burn him! Burn him!"

And so the Fire Spirit did, touching the firebrand to Zozobra's hem. The conflagration began, the skirt taking fire and spreading fiercely up the body, setting off explosions, until the huge head itself burst apart thunderously with fireworks, and the giant collapsed into ashes. Doomed, doomed, doomed.

As Jess watched, he had some sympathy for Zozobra but the phony ritual was working. Something was lifted from his dark spirits. And while the Kiwanis reps encouraged kids to come up and roast marshmallows, he reflected a bit on the meaning of it all. Here was Zozobra, who was frequently altered over the years, as he grew bigger and bigger to keep apace with contemporary appetite for the huge. And every year he was burned to the ground. Yet every year he reappeared and was always, whatever the transformations, Zozobra—his identity sustained through all the trials of metamorphosis and ruin. Jess thought about his friends—many of them, like him, rather gloomy—and how, whatever their transformations over the years and their tries at new identities, they always appeared and reappeared as . . . only themselves. He found something sustaining in this.

And he thought back to that Halloween nightmare of fiery skeletons he had when sleeping next to Natalia and Gilah so many years ago. He had been filled with unimaginable fear and anguish. But these seem to have lifted as Zozobra went up in smoke.

As he and Sinead departed the park, he knew with all his being that he would never again disappear into a world elsewhere, that Fergus was forever gone, and that he and Sinead were, like their parents, forever together.

EPILOGUE

Flying back to New York, Jess felt some problems were resolved but others were not. "We can't have sex, we can't get married, what are we going to do?" he asked Sinead.

She knew. "You buy out all the other tenants, and we adopt as many children as possible."

Eureka. Jess sensed right away that this would be the best redress for his never being up to standard for adoption as a kid.

Within a few months they bought out the entire five-floor townhouse on Bank Street and began the usually arduous process of adoption. They had an easier time of it because they were in search of medically fragile children with minority backgrounds, children usually difficult to place. Restrictions were waived by agencies and family court judges because of their large incomes and the ample housing they could offer. Sinead, who held onto her studio at Westbeth, had in mind the ministry of Prometheus, bringing light and learning into the world to alleviate man's dark estate.

They did some human engineering too. This was Sinead's idea— to adopt children from nationalities and ethnicities infamous for killing one another. They adopted an Israeli boy and a Palestinian girl, an Irish Catholic girl and a Protestant boy from Ulster, a Chechen-rebel boy and a Muscovite girl, a Sunni girl and a Shiite boy and a Kurdish child of ambiguous sex, a Pakistani girl and an Indian girl, and a Southern Indiana girl and a Northern Indiana boy. It was a miniature Global Village, and they got media attention.

"If these children can get along, why must the nations so furiously rage together?" asked Sinead of the CNN reporter.

It can't be said the children always got along. There were frequent territorial disputes—only four bathrooms and some bedrooms larger than others. "You took another piece of bacon, I saw that! Mommy, she hid a piece of bacon under her plate!" "Why does *he* get two digital robots and I've got only one?" But no blood spilt. It was a promising experiment in communal living.

Earlier, upon their return from Santa Fe, when Amanda was confronted with the real-life Jess, something happened to the quality of her feelings, as she confessed to him one evening over oysters at North Square restaurant. Not that she didn't have feelings for him still, but Eros had taken flight. She was sorry and didn't fully understand it herself. It wasn't simply that their brief try at real-life sex was lackluster. As best she could explain it, she had burned her candle at both ends, like Vincent, and now she seemed to have exhausted her fuel for both sex and love. She had decided against any campaign to become Jess's spouse, especially with Sinead hovering nearby, and she was moving on.

"It's okay with me if we change our love for friendship," said Jess. "Maybe friendship is sturdier. We don't need sex."

For other reasons, Jess was relieved, for he knew that real flesh and blood could not compete with what had been for Amanda a long carnival of the digital imagination. To be sure, her digital world had failed to blunt the age-old human drives of sex, jealousy, and will to power. Amanda too remained only human, whatever her professed indifference to the standard protocols of romance. As things now stood, he thought of her like an amphibian, with others of her generation poised between stubbornly implanted human drives and a technology that both facilitated these drives and rendered them meaningless. Why pursue with heart and soul what you can now have with a click of the mouse? Now it appeared that, emptied out, she desired to desire. Jess remembered from his core curriculum at Harvard that Samuel Johnson built an entire unreadable Eastern tale around this very dilemma.

After lifting her siege on Jess, Amanda didn't return to cyberspace. She told Jess she had enough of nerve.com and sex with strangers—it bummed her out. She gave him some credit for this— her single-minded attachment to him, even at a distance, made her rethink how she went about affairs of the heart. So the ending to her Edna St. Vincent Millay how-to book took a dark moralistic turn in matters of sex. Vincent herself had recoiled from fuck overdose. Despite objections from her editor, Amanda quoted Shakespeare, "Th' expense of spirit in a waste of shame is lust in action." Her book, *Millay for Today*, became a bestseller and was made into a pseudo-documentary starring Amanda as Vincent. She didn't look the part but performed with great esprit, and often got together with Bentley to tell stories of the actor's life.

After a period of recovering from her entanglement with Jess, Amanda looked over a fragmentary list of old boyfriends to see if anybody jogged her memory, and she got back in touch with Sergei. He had given up identity theft for venture capital and repaid all the Upper East Side widows he'd conned and all the people whose identities he'd stolen. And he apologized to Horace for having been a prick-tease. As Amanda explained it to Jess, they had much in common as penitents and millionaires. It was hardly heated romance or deep love, but they were the first of this cast of characters to get married. They bought the townhouse across the street from Jess and Sinead where Charles Kuralt had lived, and were frequent visitors. It seemed enough to freeload the adopted children, so they remained childfree themselves. Jess hoped that Amanda had not sold herself short. She told him her career was getting back on track after a period of writer's block.

Jess also worried greatly when Horace had to have his stomach staples removed because of a chronic infection. He mushroomed to his previous girth in a matter of months. But such was their bond that Bentley didn't mind. They remained steadfast, and Bentley, who always liked taking on impossible roles, took on lover-of-a-fat-man.

They too prospered. Horace switched from representing doctors to representing victims of doctors and garnered increased revenue for his increased morality. Bentley finally achieved fame as an actor when the Pearl Theatre production of Oscar Wilde's *An Ideal Husband* moved to Broadway and he was kept on as lead. With their combined income they bought the townhouse on Bank Street where feisty, hat-festooned Bella Abzug had lived in the days when there was still hope that all power is to the people. Jess, Sinead, Bentley, Horace, Amanda, and Sergei headed up the Bank Street Block Association and, in league with the New York Landmarks Preservation Commission, fought hard for removal of all modern excrescences from building façades, restoring them to their original designs.

Things went well in the fourth Greenwich Village townhouse— the house on Bethune Street. When her mother died, Natalia seemed to Jess and others freed up from yet more rules. She stopped going to Saturday afternoon confession, spending that time instead as a Greenwich Village tour guide. She was quite religious about it. And then there was fusion food. She had lost that battle worldwide. But instead of simply admitting defeat, she sent forth a new culinary concept: *fission* food. Oppenheimer had given fission a bad rap, she claimed on one of her internationally broadcast cable network shows, where she became the Julia Child for a new generation of people hoping to hold their families together through the power of cooking.

The concept of fission food was all the more powerful because, like deconstruction, nobody knew what it meant. It was unclear, for example, why Polish-Caribbean food was fission, not fusion, but Natalia Wojciechowski's authority was enough to carry the day. She frequently walked up to Jess and Sinead's house to cook fission meals for the entire company, seated at a table for twenty in the large dining room. Food fights were not uncommon, because fission food lends itself to flinging, but these were celebratory occasions, and Auntie Nattie was loved by all.

Her relationship with Irma—aka Margaret Epstein, aka Gilah de Champigny—only deepened over the years on Bethune Street. A year after Jess returned from Santa Fe, Irma asked him to remove her implants. This he did and, with the help of some old photographs that she had earlier declined to give him, Jess reworked her face. Her features were then almost completely restored to the long equine face that had first won Natalia's heart, soul, and body. Nattie was relieved she was no longer living with a dish sought out by all, or somebody whose personal vanity got them both into so much trouble. Irma happily resumed her work at Claremont Riding Stable and enjoyed giving free riding lessons to Sinead and Jess's children—at least those not so medically fragile they couldn't get on a horse. For them she purchased an antique horse from the very carousel in Central Park that Jess, Horace, and Christo had ridden that day in early spring so many years earlier. Her line of Gilah de Champigny beauty products maintained a steady large income, but the infomercials featuring her were all reruns—she no longer looked the part.

Irma was happy with her new life, and this gave Jess an idea about his own medical practice. He developed a new specialty—his practice was now confined to what he termed *cosmetic retrofusion*. It was surprising how many people lined up to have their old features restored. Instead of rhinoplasty, he did re-rhinoplasty, and restored the nasal bump that people thought they detested but then found themselves the lesser for no longer having. Not for everybody, surely, but he won a well-defined niche in the annals of plastic surgery and would be written up as a truly seminal figure, whatever his botches of yore.

It was in response to all this good fortune in the face of adversity that Sinead's sculpture gradually shifted from the agonized human form to pastoral landscape. She began doing installation art of Irish landscapes, using the literal material—earth, grass, clover, bushes—that, through special exemption by the Irish government, she imported to the States. These she took from Fermanagh in the North and Sligo in the South, the two counties where Jess and her biological parents traced their ancestry. One of these was fashioned of material taken from the banks of Lough Erne, the planet's most beautiful lake. And in the tall grass she shaped the imprint of two lovers who had recently departed, because, as Yeats writes, "the mountain grass cannot but keep the form where the mountain hare has lain."

Jess and Sinead now lived, they knew, a post-sexual kind of life. But sex became for them not just the act of getting it on—there was sex everywhere, from the food they ate to the luxuriant trees of Bank Street and the blooming of the Shakespeare Garden in Central Park to the people, young and old, who walked the sidewalk outside, often laughing and taking pleasure in the ivy that festooned their townhouse. There was sex in the novels they read and the plays they saw and the music they heard. Though they didn't declare for celibacy—and had a non-jealousy pact, admittedly fragile, should literal sex come along someday—they didn't much miss the nasty.

Natalia and Irma, and Horace and Bentley took advantage of Connecticut's 2008 legalization of same-sex marriage. They made the pilgrimage to New Haven one day where Jess gave away Horace to Bentley and Amanda gave away Natalia to Irma. Or was it the other way around? Who cares? At the wedding party afterward, held at the Yale University Commons and catered by an artisanal fission-food platoon, Jess and Sinead sang ballads of the Irish Rebellion of 1798, Sergei sang "Cossack Lullaby" and "Song of the Volga Boatmen," and Amanda gave her Michael Jackson dance riff atop the dining table.

* * *

One evening in early October, 2008 they all reconvened at Café Loup on West Thirteenth Street. Jess and Sinead, Natalia and Irma, Amanda and Sergei, Horace and Bentley—four modern couples. To Jess it seemed forever since he had first met Natalia that early October evening in 1989 in this very restaurant. What a wealth of events had rippled out from that meeting! There were some differences now—a somewhat different circle of epicures and the years they had all clocked. And this time they liked the food.

"Those escargots are so savory. The garlic must be fresh from Marseilles," said Bentley.

"Your New Zealand lamb is succulent, tender, vibrant," said Irma.

"These tournedos are to die for," said Natalia. "This bodes well for the chocolate soufflé."

It was unclear if there were a new chef or if palates grew more lenient over the years.

It was a few weeks since they'd all been together and there was much to talk about and be grateful for. For one thing, Amanda had a new book contract.

"It's with Bantam—a how to write a how-to book. It's for a much more specialized audience than *Millay for Today*."

"How'd you land that contract?" asked Sinead suspiciously. Jess too wondered if Amanda had gone back on her marriage vows.

"It's my perfect track record—one for one. I know it sounds dumb, so I'm writing a book on Hegel next. No publisher in sight. Also one on sex addiction. That one already has five bidders. Stay tuned . . . Sergie here has had some recent successes of his own, right Sergie?"

Seated as far away as possible from Horace and wearing button-fly dungarees and an unraveled sky-blue sweater as befits the recently rich, Sergei said, "I've ventured some capital in anti-cell-phone technology. I suggest you all invest . . . Pardon me, gotta take this."

A handsome young man passed by their table. "Are you by chance the famed restaurant reviewer Natalia Wojciechowski?"

Natalia beamed and said yes, while Jess and Irma squirmed, fearing a whole new cycle of misadventures. This time Horace didn't ask the gent to join them, and he slunk off.

"Maybe you should resume wearing disguises," said Jess.

"As you well know, I don't do that anymore—no longer the hard-ass reviewer. And anyway we're sending our ratings to Zagat—we need to help these old-fashioned restaurants. No disguises. Like the rest of you, I've decided to mine own self be true."

"I'm with you there, Nattie," said Sinead. "There's so much blather about reinvention and performative crossing of gender boundaries and how biology doesn't matter a hoot because everything is social construction. I'd rather construct my installation art than reconstruct me. Bentley, you're an actor, maybe you disagree."

"No. I do my reinvention on stage, and I'm convinced that all the world is *not* a stage. It's more like a pit, and instead of players we are all workers."

"If I could chime in on this," said Horace, "when I was a skinny man I felt a fat man was living within trying to get out. And now he's out where he was in the first place, and I'm me again. Bentley likes me the way I am. I inspired his Falstaff at Shakespeare in the Park, right, Bentley? . . . Could you lend me just a bite of the tournedos, Nattie?"

"And Nattie likes me the way I am," said equine Irma. "I'm grateful, Jess, that your surgeries didn't hold. Who would have guessed?"

"It's one thing I like about modern living," continued Horace. "We never know what will happen next, we don't have a clue. But I've got an announcement. Bentley and I are going to Santorini—you know, the lost isle of Atlantis—next month, but only if a donkey can be booked sturdy enough to carry me up the hill from the dock."

Horace began laughing at his own little joke. He shouldn't have been chewing steak at the same time because all at once he was quiet and lurched forward, then leaned back, putting his hands to his throat. Everyone stared at him as if paralyzed and then at the doctor. Jess knew his old friend was choking and, rather than wait for waiters to read the instructions posted on the wall, he leapt up to do the Heimlich maneuver. The problem was that Horace's girth prevented Jess from getting his arms around the waist to jolt the upper abdomen.

"Sergei, lock arms, hold him there. Bentley, you push up on our fists from the front—fast!"

Horace's bulk was such that the two men almost let him drop forward. All would have been lost, but Amanda, Natalia, Sinead, and Irma intervened, with eight arms shoving to keep the fat man upright, while Bentley thrust again and again. No result. Again, nothing. This was spoiling everybody else's dinner, as patrons helplessly looked on.

More than a couple of minutes passed, and Horace was turning purple when Jess cried, "Come on! All at once, give it everything, now!"

Out popped the tournedos.

All eight diners collapsed in their seats, the other patrons broke out in applause, and dinner continued, the waiters relieved that somebody knew the maneuver. Horace slowly caught his breath and regained color while everybody else at the table remained white.

"That would have been an awkward bow," he said weakly. "Thanks, Jess, thanks, Bentley, thanks to you all."

"Don't mention it," said Jess.

"Reminds me how good it is to stay alive," said Horace, "as if anybody here needs a reminder. Look, here comes the waiter with the soufflé!"

In light of the near catastrophe, the waiter said management was treating them to a bottle of champagne—and, by the way, please make sure the gentleman doesn't choke on his chocolate.

It fell to Jess to offer a toast. He took a deep breath and held his goblet. "Well, folks, it doesn't take a philosopher to see that we have much to be grateful for, starting with the life of Horace here."

"Yes," said Bentley, "we might have been lugging his guts to the morgue."

"That would have been a real downer," said Jess. "But we've all stuck together through thick and thin, a kind of tribal loyalty. Yeah, we've had our jealousies, our territorial fights, our illusions, but we're all still here. So let's drink to all the happy couples. May our good fortune continue and might I suggest we all reconvene as soon as Horace and Bentley return from Santorini!"

"There's one couple not here," said Irma. "Have you ever heard from your parents? It was weird to go all the way to Lobo mountain and never hear from them again."

"No word," said Sinead. "We sent cards on two Saint Patrick's Days but they didn't respond. Well, it's enough to have found them. It did us both a great deal of good—and Amanda, I guess we have you to thank."

"Not a problem. And you never know, I might put you in one of my bestsellers. Then I'll be thanking *you*."

* * *

Natalia and Irma left for Bethune Street, and the others walked quietly back to their enclave on Bank Street. Nothing like a near-death experience to chasten glib talk. Jess and Sinead said goodbye to the others and walked up the staircase to their townhouse. They had left their brood with three babysitters from P.S. 61. There was late-night noise of the various tribes and ethnicities duking it out, and maybe that's why nobody had responded to the Express Mail deliveryman. The package was sitting in the entryway.

Sinead picked it up as they stepped into the vestibule. Normally, she would have waited until they checked out the kids and paid the babysitters, but there was something that compelled her to open this package. The return address read *Kenny/Mullen, Lobo Peak, Taos, NM 87571.*

"Wonder what they've sent us, Jess. It's a little scary."

"Just pull it open. Let's see." Jess too was scared.

Out fell a hardcover onto the rug. The back of the book jacket had a photo of Emer and Tyrone standing outside their cabin in springtime. Tyrone was wearing his cowboy duds, Emer was barefoot in her Isadora Duncan tunic and scarf. They looked older but were smiling, with no apparent bruises. The dog bones had been picked up and the earthen jars looked in good repair. Jess assumed the bull terrier had died.

He and Sinead looked more closely. Both Emer and Tyrone were wearing wedding rings.

They turned the book over. The title read *With Jackrabbits: A Memoir of Life in the Old Southwest* by Emer Kenny and Tyrone Mullen, as told to Amanda Morley. It was published by Iguana Books, a distinguished Canadian house.

"My God! Amanda kept this a secret!" cried Jess.

They opened it and read the dedication: *To our children, Sinead Macantsaoiel and Jess Freeman.*

The copy was inscribed in a shaky hand, which they guessed to be Emer's, though it was signed by both.

You children gave us the summer of '61 once more, the summer when days were long and life was without ending, the summer when we gave you life too, the summer of jackrabbits and love and tall green grass by the water. We've not forgotten, and through our weary Irish hearts we dedicate to you this memoir of our lives in the old Southwest, of our brilliant careers, and of our tarnished joys. May you two forever prosper. Ty and Em.

P.S. Bibbles is still with us, making a fuss as always, with a fresh litter of five pups.

A sneak peek at Larry Lockridge's upcoming novel

The Woman in Green

In the final metafarcical novel of The Enigma Quartet, *a grouchy narrator repeatedly insults his readers of 2050 and wishes he were instead addressing readers of 2025, when somewhat fewer were boneheads. Born under a curse at the exact moment of the 9/11 attacks, he looks back at the two remarkable utopian experiments in early nineteenth-century New Harmony, Indiana, and then ahead to his grandfather Sam Coverdale's visionary effort in the millennial year, 2000, to create a new "Boatload of Knowledge" on the banks of the Wabash. His cast of characters bears a notable resemblance to Mary Shelley's circle of Frankenstein intimates. What could go wrong? From a macabre scroll found under a labyrinth to a dramatic fiasco on the world stage to a heady balloon ride to freedom, these characters plus one prescient turtle undergo one trial after another. But they hang on together as friends and lovers, averting suicide within the ranks and emerging with lasting romantic bonds and a vision that the enigmatic Woman in Green will someday prosper on Planet Earth.*

— Chapter One —

THE LABYRINTH

Nobody had ever asked what might be *under* the labyrinth. Dead center, in a small circular shrine, was a broad limestone slab bearing the angel Gabriel's footprint. Near midnight, April 1, 2000, Mary and Percy Schiller crowbarred the slab aside and peered with carbide lanterns down a narrow vertical chasm.

"Just as I expected, a tunnel," said Percy, adjusting the scrunchie on his ponytail.

"More like a sinkhole. Could swallow you up—"

"I'll go down, do a quick survey. Fasten the rope to that pedestal, Mary."

She fidgeted with the ring on her middle finger and fastened the rope. Percy grabbed it and made his way down. After ten feet, the tunnel opened into a low-ceilinged cellar, dank and redolent of rotten wood. Alighting on mud, Percy beheld large barrels stacked about the circumference. Moldy beams supported a broad-timbered roof. Crawdads scuttled in standing pools. A passageway led off to the east.

"Just as I expected—Rapp's whiskey. Mary, come on down."

She sighed and slid down the rope. The two peered at faded black letters on the barrels. *Vater Rapp me fecit, anno* MDCCCXX. Percy shook a barrel. It sloshed. He cupped a hand beneath the spigot and caught some pungent liquid. A teetotaler, he licked his fingers gingerly. "George will tell us how good it is . . . Look over there." He pointed to an elaborate apparatus. "Just as I expected, alchemical equipment."

Mary took greater interest in this, brushing aside cobwebs from the coiled tubes and old bottles filled with brackish fluid. One bottle, which resembled a Steuben decanter, stood out. In it floated two lumpy specimens the size of small plums.

"I knew we'd find them," said Percy. "Let's see what's down the passageway. A shrine, no doubt."

"You first, Parsifal."

After crouching along a few yards amid indignant bats and beetles, they emerged into another chamber, smaller but more decorative, with crude pebbly mosaics of angels and roses. They confronted an imposing piece of furniture.

"Yes, a shrine," said Percy. "A Shaker cabinet but made to order. Rapp wanted a shrine, not storage for knives and forks."

Two skeletons were neatly laid out on each side. He quickly examined teeth, skull, and hipbones. "Hmmm... male *Homo sapiens*, early forties, probably Amerindian." He inspected the shrine, made of hard pine and festooned with holy artifacts. "Hmmm... seven pewter candlesticks." The centerpiece was a naïve painting on wood, much damaged by wormholes. "That's from the Book of Revelation—the woman dressed in white."

"More like green slime."

Near the bottom of the shrine was a small vault emblazoned with innards of geodes and closed with an ornamental wax seal. "We'd better come back with the seal remover," said Percy. "A prophecy inside, if I know Father Rapp."

A congregation of unhappy bats chose not to share their dungeon with humans. *Swoosh!* The turbulence extinguished both lanterns.

Percy started to explain his hunch about the prophecy. His hunches were always right. Mary interrupted. "Look, Perse, have you noticed? We're in the dark. Do you mind? Let's get out of here!"

The Woman in Green is the final novel of *The Enigma Quartet*, following *The Cardiff Giant*, *The Great Cyprus Think Tank*, and *Out of Wedlock*. It will be released by Iguana Books on January 5, 2023.